GROVE

This is Book Three in the Trilogy.

Will the Egan curse finally be addressed? The first two books "LOOKING FOR SHONA and "THE HURT OF YOCHANA and now "GROVE" take the reader on an unforgettable journey of time travel, romance, history, good and evil.
You decide what is right and what is real as Daniel Egan sets out on the path to uncover the family's heartaches.
This book is based around the fictitious Scottish village of Grove near Paisley.
Come with Daniel and see if you can work out good from bad and how it affects his life.

Daniel didn't ask for this but now he has got it what does he do?
Let the story begin!

GROVE

My gratitude, as always, to my editor Gill Barr-Colbeck, and to a good friend and excellent cover designer Martyn Wright. Thank you for your hard work.

GROVE

This book is a work of fiction.
Names, characters, organisations,
places, events and incidents are
either products of the author's
imagination or are used fictitiously.

GROVE

Contents

GROVE

CHAPTER ONE

It was three years since Daniel's mother had passed away. Daniel sat with his parents two diaries as he had done many times. Daniel had left school, but the death of his mother had an adverse effect on him. He had fallen in with the wrong crowd and had been cautioned for marijuana possession. Although a very rich young man due to his mother's death he had squandered most of the money. All that was left was the house across from Millie.

Millie had tried to be supportive of Daniel but she was getting on in years and the worry had taken its toll on the once vivacious Millie. Daniel would promise to go and see Aunty Millie but most times he wouldn't turn up, he would be with friends or hanger-

on's, as Millie would call them.
Today he knew he had to be there for
Millie as she was going for her test
results at the hospital, and although
she was putting a brave face on
things, he knew poor Millie was very
worried.

Daniel put his cereal bowl in the now
overcrowded sink and got dressed.
Daniel's dress sense was what would
have been called Grunge years ago.
He had a blue tee shirt with a picture
of Kurt Cobain on the front, black
skinny jeans and a pair of converse
baseball shoes that had really seen
better days. His coat was a black
Crombie three quarters length coat.
He didn't wash his hair which was
naturally curly, it was just beyond
shoulder length and his beard
completed the scruffy look. With a
piece of toast in one hand he grabbed
the keys to his car, locked the house

door and walked across the road to
Millie's house.

Since Millie had been ill the garden
she loved so much had become quite
overgrown. Daniel hadn't been over
to help, so nothing was getting done.
Millie answered the door. Daniel was
a bit shocked, she appeared to have
lost even more weight.

"I'm ready Daniel."

Millie had a black coat with scarf
depicting Van Gogh paintings, she
was always well dressed. Once in
Danny's car, Danny noticed Millie's
left arm was trembling.

"Are you ok, Aunty Millie?"

"Yes, I will be fine. Just not
sleeping well and this thing started
two days ago," she said pointing to
her left hand.

Millie felt too unwell to remark on the
state of Daniel's car. The passenger
foot well was full of McDonald's

wrappers but that was Daniel at the moment. Millie was hoping he would grow out of it and that it was just a phase. Her concern was he hardly knew his mother whose death had hit him really hard.

They arrived at the hospital and as usual her appointment with Doctor Malik was running almost one and a half hours late. Eventually Malik called Millie and Daniel into his office.

"Please take a seat Mrs Trench."

"This is my godson Daniel, Doctor Malik."

"Pleased to meet you young man."

"Right your test results."

Malik opened the folder containing the results. Millie's heart was thumping, she squeezed Daniel's hand.

"I am pleased to tell you your blood tests came back positive, nothing untoward at all. Have you been under a lot of stress lately? This can quite often trigger our bodies to shut down as a kind of defective mechanism? I just noticed your hand shaking Mrs Trench."

"This only started two days ago."

"This is all very strange. Would you like me to prescribe some anti-depressants, they will help you sleep as well?"

"No, I will be fine Doctor. Maybe I need a holiday."

"Best tonic going, a bit of sunshine. If the hand shaking persists for a further month make an appointment to see me. Well unless you have any further questions I best carry on with my rounds."

Doctor Malik stood up and showed Millie out. As Daniel went past Malik shook his hand.

"Take good care of Mrs Trench, young Daniel." Daniel smiled and Malik went on his way.

"What a lovely man, eh Daniel? I feel so relieved, I really thought there was something seriously wrong with me."

"Why don't you call Aunty Jenny in Liverpool and have a holiday with her?"

"Oh, I don't know. Jenny has a lot on with the café and the kids, she probably would not want to."

"If you don't ask you won't know, will you?"

"I'll think about it Daniel, just get me home please." Daniel dropped Millie off and she opened her front door a wave of disappoint came over her. How did life get like this? Liam, Joan and Jayne dead, Daniel going through his crazy years, and her beloved Jamie not here for her to lean on.

Millie put her bag on the leather sofa and broke down crying. Her hand was shaking, she felt tired all the time.

Maybe Daniel was right, a holiday might be the answer. Millie pulled herself together and rang Jenny.

"Hi Jen, how are you?"

"Oh Millie, I was only thinking about you today then you ring, brilliant. How are you?"

"Well that's why I rang Jen, I have a few health problems."

"Not serious is it Millie?"

"No, I don't think so. I wondered if you fancy a holiday with me."

"I could do a week Millie. I have good lady that helps with the café so she should be ok. Dump would love to take Bridie and Clodagh to see his mum in Ireland, so that won't be a problem."

"I have to smile when you say your husband's name."

"Yeah everyone does Millie, great name isn't it? Flippin' Dump he loves his name. If we could go next week the girls are on school holidays so that would be perfect."

"Anywhere you fancy?"

"Not bothered Millie, you choose."

"Right, well I am excited now Jenny. I will sort something today for a week and let you know."

Millie came off the phone and started trawling the internet. She finally settled on Costa Adeje in Tenerife because that would almost certainly guarantee some sunshine. Millie phoned Jenny back just to confirm she was happy with that and the fact they would fly out on Saturday for a week.

"It's a five star bed and breakfast Jen. I prefer to go out for meals, are you ok with that?"

"Absolutely Millie, where do we fly from?"

"Manchester 8.30am and return the following Saturday at 5.45pm into Manchester."

"That's great Millie, I will see you there. How are you getting to Manchester?"

"I will get Daniel to drop me off and pick me up."

"Ok looking forward to it."

Millie confirmed the booking and spoke with Daniel. He said he would have no problem with taking and picking Millie up. After Millie left, Daniel sat again with his granddad's diary and his mother's diary He looked up Paisley on the internet, then St Matthew's Church in a place called Grove. Grove was indeed three miles out of Paisley. Daniel decided when he dropped Millie at Manchester airport he would drive up. He wanted to tell Millie, but he knew she would worry so he thought with her current health state he had best do this alone. Saturday arrived and Daniel made sure the diaries were hidden from

Millie as he put her suitcase into the boot.

"What are you doing? I see you have an overnight bag. Are you stopping in Manchester with some friends Daniel?"

"Yeah that's the plan."

"Do you need some money?"

"No, I'm fine Aunty Millie, thank you."

"Just be a good lad while I'm away, won't you?"

Millie wittered on all the way to Manchester Daniel knew she meant well but he had this church thing on his mind. Daniel dropped Millie and headed to Paisley. He figured it would be early afternoon when he arrived. Daniel's sat nav was spot on it was it was 2.20pm when he arrived in Paisley he then took a B road to Grove.
As Daniel drove into the outskirts of Grove the village sign was a bit tatty

and the grass verges hadn't been cut in decades and they were very overgrown. Daniel could see the church, it didn't have a spire. It was more like the Saxon churches that he had seen in England. The church was on the outskirts of the village and he could see a dusty road leading to some small cottages, but there didn't seem to be any life anywhere. Daniel parked his car outside the broken church gates that somebody had attempted to lock unsuccessfully. There was a big old oak tree by the side of the church. None of the graves appeared to have been tended to he thought. Daniel was feeling a little nervous as he walked up the stone flags to the church door. It was now 3.10pm. He tried the door several times but it was locked. Now unsure what to do he looked at the piece of paper that he had written the numbers he had found on images of Drigden

Schlup Concentration Camp arch. The first two were 4 and 8 with the final two 3 and 5. Daniel was shaking as he put the numbers away. He stood for a second thinking how would he get in the church when from nowhere an old lady very stooped with old clothes and a black shawl round her shoulders appeared.

"You will need this," she said stretching out her hand. In the palm of her hand was a wrought iron key quite large and heavy.

"Who are you?" Daniel said.

"I am the keeper of the key. Now you have that responsibility," and she just disappeared. Daniel turned and fumbled pushing the key into the rusty lock. Eventually the big door opened with a loud squeaking noise. The church inside was immaculate but just as if time had stood still. Daniel walked between the old pews arriving at the altar. Behind the pulpit was a picture Daniel took as John The Baptist. It's now or never he thought. Daniel hesitated. The diary had said for certain that once he knew the truth that he would die. Surely this could not all be true he thought or was he just trying to convince himself.

He removed the picture and placed it at the bottom of the steps to the pulpit. Sure enough there was a safe. He clicked the numbers four then eight followed by three and eventually with his hand shaking he turned the dial to the final number which was five. The safe mechanism seemed to hesitate. It eventually opened the safe but then there was also a door. Daniel took out the key that had been left by Maria Klinck. This opened the final door to give access to what lay inside the safe. There were two manuscripts. Daniel took them out and blew the dust off them. He sat at one of the pews and started to look at the script.

'Bejla'e' ts'o'ok sido yéeyik utia'al u xu'ulul yéetel le nuumyaj yóok'ol kaab. U u le ken jóok'okene' le kúuchila' ku toj ka' u manuscrito ti' u sajak u beel ts'o'ok u yéeyik'. All the writings were in a language he didn't understand so he decided to get a hotel for the night and see if he could translate on the internet. Daniel closed the safe, locked the first door and re-entered the numbers then put back the picture of John The Baptist and headed to the car, locking the church on the way. It was starting to get dark as he drove down through what he expected to be a village but was nothing more than a very small hamlet. He passed three houses on the left, then what looked like a derelict pub on the right, then nothing other than crumbling cottages where the road came to a dead end. Daniel turned the car round and headed back the way he came hoping to find accommodation in Paisley.

Paisley was famous as the birth place of William Wallace so it was no surprise to see a hotel called The William Wallace. Daniel took out his overnight bag and headed off towards the reception. A bright young Scottish girl greeted him.

"Good evening Sir, how can I help you?"

"I wondered if you have a room for a couple of nights?"

"Yes, we do Sir. Would you like en-suite?"

"Oh yes please."

"Ok Sir that will be two hundred and twenty two pounds for the two nights including breakfast. Breakfast is served from 7.00am until 9.30am. If you have any special requests just let me know and I can make sure the kitchen staff accommodate you. You are on the second floor, room 201, Sir."

"Thank you. What do people do for nightlife round here?"

"If you go out of the hotel lobby and turn left you will come to Proud Square, there are number of bars and restaurants there."

"Ok thank you."

The young lady smiled at Daniel, although going through his Grunge look, he still had his mother and grandma's looks which certainly had turned the head of the young lady on reception. Armed with the hotel wifi code Daniel tried to decipher the language in the manuscripts. After almost two hours he finally cracked the written language, it was Yucatec Maya. The opening words were **'Now you have been chosen to end the world's misery. Be sure when you leave this place that you follow the**

**manuscript in its entirety, your
path has been chosen'**
Daniel didn't know what it all meant
but he did feel anxious. He decided to
go and get a drink and then spend the
following day translating the rest of
the books. He smiled at the
receptionist has he left the hotel. He
turned left and headed for Proud
Square. Daniel walked into a small
pub called the Green Tankard and
ordered a pint of bitter.

"You mean a pint of heavy,
laddie," said a guy sat at the bar.
Daniel looked a bit bemused. The
Scotsman laughed.

"It's what we call beer up here son,
dunna take offence. I'm Murdo," and
he thrust out his hand.

"Daniel, pleased to meet you
Murdo. Would you like a drink with
me?"

"That's very kind of you. I'll have
a large Dewey."

With the drinks now served Daniel sat chatting with Murdo.

"What brings a young Sassenach ta bonny Scotland?"

Daniel wasn't going to say the real reason so he made a story up that he was tracing family history.

"Ya family is from Paisley eh?" the Scotsman said.

"Well near here, Grove."

Murdo was just taking a swig from his beer and nearly choked.

"Bloody hell, Grove. You want to keep away from Grove if you have any sense laddie."

"Why is that?"

"Do you not know the story?"

"No, what story?"

"Well legend has it that an Irish family moved there in 1497. The town was thriving but they had a really bad winter for the months of January, February and early March. The snow was relentless, many died through starvation, they were cut off from the outside world. Those that did survive noted that the Irish family had seemed fine they appeared to have food and clothes and wood for their fire. Questions were beginning to be asked how could a wretched Irish family afford or be able to get provisions. Everyone who lived in the village worked at the coal mine, it was arduous work in those days, all pick and shovel. Men met their deaths regularly so widows were common in Grove. The men tried to work the mine through the harsh conditions, again many were killed. Before the Irish family arrived they were reputed to be three hundred and eight men, women and children. By the end of 1497 there were sixty seven of the original town folk that had survived or not moved on. Rumblings were that the Irish family were servants of the devil. The local landlord a Mr

William Brewster, told the head of the
Irish family to leave his ale house
saying no devil worshipper was
welcome in his establishment. It is
said Dermot Egan looked at him and
the whites of Egan's his eyes shone
blood red."

"Sorry did you say Dermot Egan?"

"Yes, I did Laddie why?"

Daniel felt coldness run down his
spine.

"Oh I just wondered, I went to
school with somebody called Egan."
The Scotsman carried on with his
story.

"Two days later Brewster was
found hung in his orchard. The
remaining people were scared and
nobody now questioned the Egan
family. If they saw them in the street
they would hurry about their
business."

"Surely that's a load of rubbish,"
Daniel said.

"Well if it was, the story has survived to the present day. There were many incidents in the village of Grove. The next instance was a few weeks later. Malky McAndrew had been to market with two pigs. On his way home he called at The Tumbling, a small ale house, some two miles from the market in Socombe. Socombe had a reputation for witchcraft, two local women had been burned at the stake the previous month. On entering the Ale House McAndrew ordered his ale but then saw in the corner Dermot Egan talking to a local girl, Ellie Fairbury. Ellie worked at the The Tumbling and McAndrew knew her parents. Egan was getting fresh with her and she was trying to avoid his advances. McAndrew was quite a nasty tempered man. He didn't believe all the superstitions about the Egan family and he wasn't about to let Ellie get man-handled by Egan, so he went across. Egan let go of Ellie and stood up. He was a big man, possibly six feet five, with hands like shovels. McAndrew ripped into him but Egan just stared at him. Again, legend has it Egan's eyes turned blood red. He never said a word and McAndrew was remonstrating with arms flailing about. Suddenly McAndrew held his left arm and appeared to start choking. They say yellow bile came out of his mouth as he fell onto the wooden floor. Egan stepped over him and whispered something in his ear whilst picking his coat up off the chair and calmly walked out. Within minutes McAndrew was dead."

"The story was soon the talk of all the towns. Fear followed Dermot Egan. He didn't physically attack anyone so no charges could be brought against him. At that time in

Paisley there was a Soothsayer called Colyne Dancourt, he had predicted many things."

"In one of his writings he said that **'a person of Irish descent would arrive in Scotland in the winter of the most horrible. Many will die from hunger; the devil family would survive. Many more are to be taken by the devil for the man is possessed. One day a fresh face man will come and he will change the course of history forever. The devil shall possess many people which will cost many lives during time of the dark days until the light doth shine again. Europe will see the devil in the form of a small man whose arm will shake and the New World will be found but many people will die fighting the devil over many centuries. There will be many instances of evil before the**

devil shall be beaten and only one man can save mankind from itself"

Daniel was concerned and wanted to get back to the hotel to write down and research what the Scotsman had said. He thanked the Scotsman, buying him a double whisky before leaving him talking to another tourist. Had Daniel not known what he knew now, he maybe would have dismissed the Scotsman and his story. But knowing what he was in Scotland for and finding that an Egan could have been possessed by the devil, was now more than just a legend for him. Back at the hotel the young lady at reception shouted hello to Daniel.

"Are you staying anymore nights?"

"Maybe book me in for another couple of nights please."

"I was only asking because my friend is having a party tomorrow night and I wondered if you would like to go with me if you have nothing planned?"

"That's kind of you. I would love to." He looked at the young girl's badge, it said Lee-Anne Tapton.

"Where shall I meet you, Lee-Anne?"

"Did you see a pub called the Diggers next to a churchyard?"

"Yes, I did see that."

"I will meet you there at 7.30pm, Daniel."

"Ok see you then," and Daniel headed to his room.

Once back in his room he noticed he had five missed calls from Millie. Oh heck he thought. He started his laptop and called Millie.

"Hey Daniel, I have been trying to get hold of you."

"Sorry Aunty Millie I have been out."

"Hope you are being a good lad."

"I am honest. How is the hotel?
Are you having a nice time?"

"It's lovely Daniel the food is
fabulous and it was 28C today. Even
better news, suddenly today my arm
stopped shaking."

Daniel started wondering if there
had been a connection with what he
was doing. He played it off by saying.

"Maybe you had a trapped nerve
Aunty Millie."

"I don't know Daniel but I feel
great again. In fact, I have not felt as
good as this since I was a teenager."

They carried on talking for half an
hour but Daniel was desperate to get
some research done. Finally Millie
said she had to go.

Daniel started writing in his diary
what had happened so far and the
conversation with the Scotsman. It
was 1.00am in the morning when

feeling tired he powered down his computer and climbed into bed. Daniel was soon asleep and he started dreaming. He could see himself as William Dowd, he looked like Daniel with curly hair. Dowd's master was Anthony Babington, a dandy of a man. Daniel could see himself bringing drinks to his master Anthony Babington at the table. He knew the others were Robert Poley, Leviathan Gifford and two other men who Dowd didn't know. Daniel was listening as they were plotting to murder Queen Elizabeth I. This can't be right Daniel thought.

"You need to write to Mary and get her permission to do this Babington," Gifford said. "You are our leader it should come from you."

This is treason of the highest order William thought. That night William hatched a plan to stop his master from doing this terrible thing.

GROVE

The following morning Babington called William from out of the kitchen.

"I want you to ride to Shugbourough forest where you will be met by a man. Ask him this question. 'Are we together?' Don't say anything else, do not engage in conversation other than those words. If the man replies, 'The Pope, The Pope' then hand over the letter. If he says anything else you are to turn your horse round and gallop steadfastly. Do not come back here. Just outside the forest there is a clearing where you will see a fast running river. Send your horse on its way and swim the river, you are young and capable. Once at the other side make a small fire and burn this letter. Do not break the seal but make sure you burn it well. You can then make your way back here. If you do not come back in one week from now

I will know you have betrayed me and retribution will fall on your family so harsh that no man would want this. Do I make myself clear?"

William nodded and a horse was brought round. On the way William was thinking what he should do. Does he report Babington to somebody? If he did would they torture him and his family as accomplices.

William lived in Dethick, a small village in Derbyshire. Life was harsh, his father had been badly injured in a hunting accident some years before and could not work. He was the eldest and had seven brothers and a sister who all relied on him.

William's heart was beating fast as he entered the outskirts of the forest. He rode for almost one hour when from nowhere three men descended on him. Remembering what Babington told him. One of the men asked who he was?

Nervously William said, "Are we together?"

"Why do you ask that? What have you in the pouch?"

William knew the game was up. He spun his horse round and rode like the wind. The three men were in hot pursuit. After ten minutes he found the river. William quickly jumped off the horse slapping it, and it disappeared into the distance. He could hear the three men approaching. William looked at the fast running river and decided it was now or never. Capture meant certain death not only for him but his poor family. Although a strong boy William was only sixteen and the current was so strong he thought he would drown. The flow took him further down the river and William disappeared under the foaming river many times before the river calmed.

William managed to swim to a sandy bank he pulled himself out of the water. His knees were bleeding and he had several cuts to his face. He scurried up the side of the sandy bank and hid. It was quiet, he couldn't hear anything except the birds singing. William decided to wait for the night before trying to make a small fire, the parchment was wet anyway. Although he had been told not to break the seal before he burnt the document, he was inquisitive to know what was written.

William sat cross legged in the long grass and with great apprehension he carefully broke Babington's seal. William was a clever lad and since the age of twelve the cook he worked with had taught him to read and write.

Basically, the letter was for Mary Stuart. William could see why the letter needed to be burnt. Babington had written that he and some close associates were going to kill the Protestant Queen and that Mary could then become Queen of England, and the rightful religion would then be restored and with a Catholic Queen. He said he wanted Mary's approval and the task would be carried out.

William was shaking as he read the letter his master had written and signed. That night it was a full moon and William made a small fire further back in the forest.
Suddenly Daniel woke from his dream. He was sweating and felt very uncomfortable as he wrote in the diary what had happened. Daniel wrote down word for word his dream and then noted the date and he stated that he wondered how this was to end. Daniel finished the writing and went down to the hotel restaurant for breakfast.

A waiter in his early thirties came over and took Daniel's order. He poured a coffee and sat thinking about the dream.

"Hello," said a voice, "may I sit with you?"

Daniel looked up and a man in his late fifties with greying dark hair and wearing a strange multi coloured jumper stood before him.

"Oh yes, sorry, by all means."

"My name is Leviathan Harkan," he said spelling each letter for Daniel in some kind of way to make Daniel not forget.

"Pleased to meet you Mr Harkan."

"Please, Leviathan, Daniel," he said.

Daniel was taken aback. How did he know his name?

"I'm sorry Sir, but how do you know my name?"

"I know your family name, Mr Egan."

"Who are you?"

"I have told you Leviathan Harkan."

Just then the waiter brought Daniel and Leviathan's breakfast.

"Thank you kindly Sir," said Harkan.

"Look I am a bit confused, how did that waiter know you were going to have breakfast at this table?"

"There are many things Daniel, that will be revealed in good time. Enjoy your breakfast."

Leviathan ate in a most awful way. Daniel thought with every mouthful he would wipe his tongue round his lips. It was quite disgusting to watch so Daniel tried hard not to stare.

"Do you like books Daniel?"

"Some, why do you ask?"

"I have a small book shop just around the corner, I could show you it if you would like?"

Not only was Daniel quite sceptical of this stranger but he was weird. Daniel declined and made his excuse and left Leviathan sitting at the table.

"I will see you again Daniel." Daniel smiled but under his breath he said, "not if I can help it."
Daniel left the hotel and went into Paisley he had decide to smarten himself up. He quite liked Lee-Anne and wanted to make a good impression, although washing his hair was not an option. He liked the Rastafarian look and anyway it had taken years to get it like it was. Not being used to clothes shopping Daniel bought a new pair of skinny chino's, a brown pair of brogues, light blue shirt and beige sports coat. That will do he thought and he headed back to the hotel.

The lure of the Green Tankard was too much, so he called in for a quick drink. At the corner of the bar he could see Murdo. Daniel shouted across, "Would you like a drink?"

"I'll have a large one and a pint of heavy with you son."

That meant a large whisky and a beer. Daniel ordered a pint and wandered over to Murdo.

"Thought you would have been well gone laddie, you must like Paisley."

"Actually, I do Murdo."

"You been clothes shopping? I see you have your eye on a wee lassie, I don't doubt?"

"Well actually Murdo, you are correct."

"Just think on laddie. Me Mammy used to say to me, when you get a girlfriend a penny bun costs yer tuppence, and she was nay far wrong. Why don't you move up here laddie if ye like it?"

"Oh, I'm not sure."

"That wee lassie has turned your head," and Murdo laughed.

"Look Murdo, I best get back and get ready for my hot date."

"Well, have a good time laddie and remember what I told yer about the cost of a bun."

Daniel laughed and left Murdo ordering another Dewey.

Back at his room he phoned Aunty Millie, he didn't say anything about what he had found out for fear of upsetting her. Millie was buoyant, and said she and Jenny were having a great time. They had been to some old ruin and were now having cocktails and nibbles at a bar. Millie sounded so much better, she told Daniel the shaking in her arm had gone completely. After a few more minutes Daniel rang off and had a shower. He left the hotel at 7.20pm and headed for the Diggers arms. The pub was a typical old Scottish pub with small alcoves everywhere, it really was quaint. Lee-Anne saw Daniel and gestured for him to come over. Lee-Anne was standing with two other couples who Lee-Anne introduced to Daniel. This is Kirsty Miles and Alan Tapper, they are engaged, and this is the birthday girl Alli Beaman, and her boyfriend Alex Crew. Daniel shook hands with everyone.

"So Daniel, what brings you to bonnie Scotland?"

"I am researching my family tree."

"Oh, my uncle did that a few years back, he got back to about 1400 I think. My seven times removed Grandad and Grandma lived in 'Grove'," Alex said in a hushed voice. Everybody reeled back in mocking manner.

"His was the local landlord called William Brewster. Apparently he died in some weird way."

Daniel quickly changed the subject.

"Nice pub," he said.

"It's always been a good pub."

"So, are you all from Paisley?"

"No, only Alex and me," said Lee-Anne.

"I'm from Cumbria," Alli Beaman said, "and Kirsty and Alan are from Yorkshire. We all met at University."

"I dropped out Daniel, I was doing my final year and it got too much, so now I work in the hotel."

"As long as you are happy Lee-Anne that's all that matters."

"I agree Daniel."

The night went well and as they all went their own way Daniel and Lee-Anne walked back to the hotel.

"Would you like a coffee in my room Lee-Anne?"

"I shouldn't really. If I get reported I will get the sack."

"Oh, come on, who will know? I'm certainly not going to tell anyone," and he laughed.

The drink took over Lee-Anne's thoughts so she stayed the night. The following morning she was up early and left Daniel sleeping. She just left a note for him with her mobile number. Daniel was in a deep sleep and back in the forest.

William had successfully burnt the parchment, and thankfully there had been no sign of the men that had chased him. He really wanted to run away because he knew one day this would end badly, but his thoughts were for his mother and father and family. Without him they would starve. William hadn't slept very well on the floor of the forest so he decided to make his way back to Dethick and the wrath of Babington. William arrived back and went downstairs where the cook, who had befriended him, gave him some broth. It was now time to go and see Anthony Babington. He found Babington pacing up and down in the great hall. There were two other men there.

"Well boy, where have you been?"

"I have burnt the letter Sir."

"What?"

William explained to the three men what had happened.

"You fool, come with me," Babington was in an awful rage.

William was taken to the stables and tied to an oak post. Babington told the stable lad to whip him until he said to stop. The poor stable boy knew William very well, but if he didn't do it he would get the same. William screamed as the lashes rained down on his young back. The blows lasted for about ten minutes. Finally Babington and the other two men agreed he had been punished enough.

"Untie the fool and leave him where he falls," and they walked away. The stable lad ran to the kitchen and asked the cook for salt. The cook came over and rubbed salt into the wounds. She nursed poor William.

"Whatever did you do to Mr Babington, Mr Poley or Mr Titchborne, young William?"

"I can't say or you will be implicated," came the reply. Poor William knew his days were numbered now.

On the 3rd September 1586 Babington and his co-conspirators were rounded up. Poley who had been a spy for Sir Francis Walsingham stood and watched as the other conspirators were taken to the Tower of London to wait a trial for treason. William, by now was very scared, but again could not leave his family as they relied on him. William Dowd decided to tell Mr Poley what he had gone through and was subsequently hung, drawn and quartered as a warning to others.

Daniel woke sweating profusely. Had he been William? It certainly felt like it. He showered and went down for breakfast. He ordered a cooked breakfast and as the previous day Leviathan Harkan appeared from nowhere.

"Hello Daniel goodnight's sleep did you have?"

"Why do you ask? Who are you?"

"I have told you Daniel. I would seriously suggest you meet me at my little bookshop on Brook Street."

With that Harkan got up and walked away. Daniel finished his breakfast and decided to do as Harkan had said. Maybe he had answers.

Brook Street was a small cobbled street about half a mile from the hotel.

GROVE

It was reputed to be the place where people were hung and crowds would gather. The street was narrow but opened up into a small area which had a circle of well-worn stone steps, six in all Daniel counted. A small plaque on a stand at the side told the story of the hangings from the steps. Behind the steps was the book shop. As Daniel nervously entered the shop a loud bell introduced the door being opened, and Daniel went inside. The shop was small, the front room was full of books. Leviathan Harkan came from the back room. He had bright maroon trousers on, with red plimsolls and another multi-coloured sweater.

"Good to see you took my advice young man," he said in a quite pompous fashion.

"Look, who are you? How do you know so much about me?"

"You have to figure that out for yourself. You have already followed the party line by getting young William Dowd hung."

"What do you mean? How do you know about my dream?"

"Daniel Egan, you have many reasons for your existence and your first reason was Babington. You chose to burn the letter. That was your choice."

"Explain to me."

"All will become clear in time."

"This is rubbish," and Daniel stormed out of the bookshop.

Once outside Daniel phoned Lee-Anne he needed some normality is his life. He knew he could not involve her but he wanted to see her.

"Hey, good morning."

"Hello Daniel, where are you?"

"Just wandering if you fancy a coffee?"

"Tell me whereabouts, then I will know where to meet you Daniel."

"I have just left Brook Street and turned onto.." Daniel paused for a minute. "Cabbage Street."

"Ok Daniel, walk up Cabbage Street and by Silvas Jewellery shop turn left. Almost immediately you will see a coffee shop called the Clootie Dumpling. I will meet you there in a few minutes."

Daniel found the coffee shop and went in. Almost immediately Lee-Anne followed him in. They were shown to a little table and Lee-Anne ordered two coffees and two Clootie dumplings.

"I am intrigued Lee-Anne, what exactly is a Clootie Dumpling?"

"It's a traditional Scottish pudding. They make it in the traditional way over an open fire, they were made before ovens were invented. They have fruit in them. There are about twenty one ways they are served, so I have ordered my favourite for me which is with warm syrup and cream. They call this the Jumbo Special and I ordered you a Clootie dumpling with cream, ice cream and Stag's breath liqueur seeing that you are on holiday, and I have to work today. They call this one Stag's breath special. The coffee and the Clootie's came out. Daniel was quite astounded.

"Blimey Lee-Anne these are massive."

"Och away with you bonnie lad, it will put hairs on yer chest," and she laughed.

"That's the first time to be honest I could tell you were Scottish."

They sat laughing and joking until 12.30pm then Lee-Anne said she had to go to work. As they walked along hand in hand Daniel felt a closeness to Lee-Anne. She was so bubbly and nice, it all felt right.

"What are you going to do for the rest of the day?"

"Thought I might go to the library and see if I can find any more about my family. What time do you finish tonight?"

"Only on until 8.00pm."

"Great, do you fancy going for a drink?"

"To be honest I would much sooner have a take-away at mine, if you want?"

"Yeah, that would be great."

Daniel kissed Lee-Anne outside the hotel and with instructions from Lee-Anne he headed for Paisley library.

Paisley Library was a Victorian building with ornate stone carvings over the entrance showing the opening date, 1867. Daniel entered the grand building and to the right through two massive oak carved doors it said 'library'. Daniel made his way over to a lady sitting at a desk who he assumed was in place to sign out the books.

"Excuse me."

The lady looked up from a book she was reading which Daniel noted to be 'Falling Leaves and Mountain Ashes'.

"How can I help you?" she said. The librarian was slight women with dark hair in a bun. She wore what Daniel thought were butterfly glasses, a bit like they wore in the early sixties in the films he had watched.

"Yes, I wondered do you have any books on the village of Grove?"

The librarian seemed a little shocked at Daniel's request, but she got up from her desk and said quite abruptly, "Follow me."

She took Daniel down several book passageways to and another area and she pointed.

"Everything on Grove is on these shelves. If you require any further help Sir, I will be at the front desk," and she turned and walked away.

Daniel started looking through the different books, and there appeared to be an author called Ewan Hufton who had written three books on Grove and its people. Daniel noted the name and decided to research Hufton back at the hotel. He thanked the librarian and left.

He was just about to walk past The Green Tankard when Murdo appeared from nowhere.

"Are you no coming in for a heavy laddie?" he said in his strong Scottish accent.

"Well I wasn't going to Murdo. I am going out with Lee-Anne tonight."

"Aw away with you, we can just have a couple, come on."

"Ok, you twisted my arm."

As usual, one became two became three.

"Murdo, I see they want bar staff here with live in accommodation."

"What you thinking about laddie?"

"Wondered about applying."

"Och you nay need apply. Billy the owner is my mate. I can have a word if you are serious."

"Yeah, what the hell."

"So, when are you going tay introduce me to your wee lassie. I am assuming that's why yer want to stay."

"Will you be in later?"

"What time?"

"We are going for a meal at eight so will be back here about 9.30pm."

"Ok laddie, I'll wait on yer and I will sort the job out for you with Billy."

"You are a star Murdo."

"Then ya best get me a Dewey laddie afor ya go."

Daniel duly obliged and left Murdo joking with a couple of his pals.

Daniel arrived back at the hotel. Lee-Anne was busy with guests so he just smiled and mouthed, "8.00pm don't be late," and he headed for the lift. He decided to shower to freshen up then sat with his laptop researching the author Ewan Hufton. Apparently Hufton had been a history professor at Paisley University until he took up writing in the early seventies. There were indeed three books he had written on Grove. Daniel wondered if he was still alive and if so, did he live in Paisley? More research followed, and he found an address for Ewan Hufton. He lived at Cragmouth, Colley Road, Paisley. Daniel was excited but also apprehensive, he wanted to meet this man to see if what he had been told could be confirmed. Lee-Anne had decided she was too tired to go out so he didn't get to introduce Lee-Anne to Murdo or find out about the job.

CHAPTER TWO

The following day Daniel drove out to the outskirts of Paisley to a small village called Cragmouth. The village consisted of a pub, a small shop, a butchers and about forty houses. Daniel thought Ewan Hufton's bungalow was the last property as you were about to leave Cragmouth. With trepidation Daniel walked up the path. The bungalow had a neat small lawn, with flower beds. To the right-hand side was a detached garage that looked like it had seen better days. Daniel knocked on the door. After a few seconds a gentleman answered the door.

"Come in Daniel, nice to meet you."

Daniel was taken back. How did Hufton know his name?

"I'm sorry Sir but how do you know my name?"

"That really doesn't matter," Hufton said, "all will be revealed in good time?"

This gets weirder by the minute Daniel thought.
Hufton showed Daniel into his living room.

"Tea and biscuits Daniel?"

"Oh err, yes please."

Hufton's living room was quite untidy. There were books everywhere stacked on shelves and then piled on the floor. Hufton arrived back with a pot of tea and two china cups and a plate of fig biscuits. Daniel hated fig biscuits. He had no choice but to eat one as he didn't want to upset Mr Hufton, he needed the information on Grove.

"So young man, how can I help you?"

"Well I am researching my family tree."

"Really," said Hufton.

Daniel was unsure what he meant by 'really', it was if he knew what Daniel was really doing.

"My ancestors were from Grove."

Hufton showed no emotion but just sat listening to Daniel.

"I saw at the local library that you had written three books on the village."

Finally Hufton began to talk.

"Daniel, before I talk about Grove you need to understand the nature of the beast."

"What do you mean?"

"The village of Grove was dammed the moment your ancestor and his family settled there."

"How could that be Mr Hufton?"

"The story of Grove intrigued me and when I started writing, the first book I wrote was on Grove. Daniel noticed Hufton's left hand was shaking like his Aunty Millie's did.

"I know things that will happen to you unless you leave Paisley. There are evil forces in Grove and you will be affected."

"Please explain to me what will happen."

"I will tell you this one thing, then I want you to leave."

Daniel was quite shocked how afraid Hufton appeared.

"Dark days are coming and you have been chosen, the path you tread will decide the future. Now Daniel leave, and never darken my door again."

Daniel was shown the door and immediately he was on the outside step, Hufton slammed the door to. What the hell was this all about Daniel thought? Lee–Anne was going to a night class. She was studying

Scottish History at night school, so
Daniel wasn't seeing her that evening
and an early night was called for.
Daniel showered and climbed into the
big bed. He had decided he was going
to see if Lee-Anne would let him
move in with her, and he would
hopefully have good news on the pub
job that Murdo was sorting.
Daniel fell asleep almost immediately.
He found himself in Derbyshire, in a
small village called Eyam. Daniel was
a butcher's apprentice in the year
1665. Daniel, or as he was called at
this time, Thomas Bent, worked six
days a week for the butcher, Mr
Snoddy. He was a big jolly red face
man who was quite nice to work for.
Thomas had heard some terrible
stories of the way apprentices were
treated, but Mr Snoddy was a kindly
employer. As long as Thomas worked
hard, and went to church twice on a
Sunday, then Mr Snoddy was kind to

him. It was August when Thomas and the villager's lives would change forever. The local travelling tailor, a Mr George Vicars, was eagerly waiting some cloth from his supplier in London. Sadly, the cloth arrived and was infested with fleas which rats carried. London was in the grip of the bubonic plague and this caused Eyam, and its village population to be decimated. Three days later Thomas was working in the back of the butcher's shop when Reverend Mompesson came in for his usual ham hock.

"Poor George Vicars has died from the fever, Mr Snoddy. I fear it's the plague."

"Do you Reverend, and what brings you to that conclusion may I ask?"

"Well Mrs Hancock, who cleaned the accommodation where Vicars was staying, said he had received cloth from London and she had seen fleas on it."

"That is terrible Reverend. Is Mrs Hancock alright?"

"I think so, but I have called a meeting at Custard Fields and I have closed the church. Be there at six o'clock to discuss what we should do."

"I will be there Reverend."

"Make sure young Thomas is with you Mr Snoddy."

"Oh, I will Reverend."
Snoddy started explaining to Thomas.

"I am frightened, Mr Snoddy."

"You need not be young Thomas. I have something that we can take every day and the plague won't touch us."

"What do you mean Mr Snoddy?"

"Look at this," Snoddy showed him a bucket of fat.

"If we drink this every day we will be safe."

"We best tell the village eh Mr Snoddy?"

"No lad we tell no-one. There isn't enough to go round and if we did tell anyone, they would probably think we had something to do with the Plague spreading, you know how people are."

"Is that the Christian way Mr Snoddy?"

Thomas hadn't seen Snoddy angry before. He clipped Thomas round the head and told him to get in the back and do some work.

At the gathering they were told that Bradshaw, the Lord of the Manor, had fled with his children. Mompesson said if anybody wanted to leave they could, but they had to go now. He said he did not blame anybody, and his children had left, but his wife was staying to help. Mompesson said he had no antidote for this most serious of events. Thomas looked at Snoddy and wanted to tell the congregation what Snoddy had said, but what if Snoddy denied it, then sacked Thomas. Thomas realised he could not tell anybody.

Two days later Mrs Hancock's first child had died and so the pattern was set. Snoddy gave Thomas a small cup of warm fat every morning and every night the same. A lot of the villagers had left and a lot had died when word was sent to the Duke of Devonshire. The village was to be effectively sealed, nobody came in and nobody went out. In return, the Duke made provisions for food to be left for the villagers for a small amount of money. This was to be left in the pools of vinegar that had been made on Custard Stone, a large stone halfway up the hill on Custard Fields. Thomas had the job of collecting money from the villagers who quite often were tending to a sick family member. Every time he went out Snoddy would say, if you tell anyone lad you won't survive this. With Snoddy's words ringing in his ears Thomas did the task he was given.

It was the middle of spring when Thomas had time to visit his parent's house. He found his mother sitting at the kitchen table crying. There were seven children, eight with Thomas who was the eldest. Jack Bent, his father, had died from the plague and his mother Mary had tended, and then buried, four of her eight children. He always gave his wages to his mother. Seeing his poor mother so upset and knowing that Snoddy appeared to have the antidote, his loyalties were torn. Did he tell his mother but then how would she get the fat in the quantity required? If he did tell her and it was a load of rubbish then he had lost the only income the family had, and nobody would employ him because Mr Snoddy would make up some cock and bull story and he would be an outcast.

The following months passed and each week more and more of the villagers died. Snoddy was well and he had come into contact with plenty of plague victims. Thomas was also well but his mum had buried the rest of the family. At times the village was like a ghost town. People didn't mingle except on a Sunday at Custard Fields where Reverend Mompesson would give a service in a morning and evening.

It was the evening sermon when Thomas started to question his faith. Why had he been chosen to live? With tears rolling down his cheek he put his arm round his mum. She tried to stop him for fear her son could get contaminated like his brothers and sisters.

The Reverend Mompesson was giving a fearsome sermon he had also just lost his wife to the plague.

"The devil is here he is among us. We must seek him out and put an end to this malevolent business. He wants you to denounce your God; his evil way will try to turn you. Don't be turned stand steadfast against the forces of evil your God will take care of you"
Some in the crowd openly questioned why some had been taken, yet some were still alive. One man pointed at Snoddy.

"Look at this man. He carries no burden, he is well. Why is this Reverend when my wife and four children have been taken from me?"

Suddenly the man started coughing
this broke up the congregation as they
fled not wanting to be contaminated.
Thomas looked at Snoddy in disgust.
Snoddy smiled, "Come on lad we
have animals to butcher."
Two days later it was pay day Snoddy
gave Thomas his wages. As he always
did, he warned him of speaking with
his mother or anyone else about the
warm fat drink. Thomas walked
through the silent village passing a
man with a make-shift wooden cart
with two bundles wrapped in cloth.
Two more of the poor man's family to
be buried. Thomas arrived at his
mother's house on the edge of the
village. Ruth Masson was standing at
the door.

"It's taken your mother Thomas.
Don't go in there or you could be
next."

Thomas fell on his hands and
knees.

"Get up," Ruth said, "You have to be a man Thomas. We all have to pull together, those of us who survive."

Thomas said nothing to Ruth and left in haste to return to Snoddy's butchers shop. There was nothing now to stop him telling the village of the drink Snoddy had concocted. Snoddy was waiting. He had already heard and knew Thomas would be wanting to tell the village. As Thomas walked into the back room Snoddy was waiting. He hit Thomas on the back of the head with a meat cleaver. He knew he could bury Thomas on the pretence he had the plague and had died.

Suddenly Daniel woke from his dream sweating and confused. He opened his laptop and realised although months had gone by in his dreams it was only 10.00am and the chambermaid was knocking on the door to clean the room. Daniel shouted for her to return in a couple of hours. He made the entries in his diary about the second dream then showered and changed. Daniel knew now that whatever his ancestors and his father had, he also had but so far his was different. He decided to meet Lee-Anne on her break and ask her about moving in and the job at the Green Tankard. Lee-Anne took him to Fort Knox a small but pleasant restaurant tucked in a side street. She said her friend Beryl Knox owned it so she always told the guests at the hotel to eat there.

Daniel finally plucked up courage to ask Lee-Anne if he could move in and about the job at the Green Tankard. Lee-Anne was so pleased she hugged Daniel

"We are meant to be," she said gushing with enthusiasm. "Oh Daniel, I am so pleased."

"Somebody looks happy?" Beryl Knox inquired as she put down two coffees and two pieces of Knox Scottish Aero Cheesecake.

"What a day I am having Beryl. See my Daniel is moving in with me and you have just placed your fantastic Knox special cheesecake in front of me. Does it get any better?"

"Aw thanks honey. Have you got a job up here Daniel?"

"I think so Beryl. I will know this afternoon."

"Where are you hoping to work?"

"The Green Tankard."

"That's a great little pub. you will be fine there. Well listen mate, best get on. We have a party of twenty six in tonight for a retirement party."

"Good luck with that then Beryl."

Lee-Anne and Daniel finished their cheesecake and coffee and Lee-Anne headed back to work. Daniel headed for the Green Tankard hopefully to get the job.

"Hey Daniel lad where have you been?"

"Sorry Murdo, Lee-Anne was tired the other night."

"Right I have spoken with Billy and you can start next Tuesday. He has given me a rota for yee."

"Murdo you are a star. Thank you so much. I am moving in with Lee-Anne tomorrow so it will give me time to nip back to London and get my clothes etc."

"Anytime wee laddie, enjoy your company and I bet I get plenty of top ups when you are on."

"You bet you will mate."
With things sorted Daniel had to pick Millie up from the airport so he was going to tell her on the way to London. Daniel met Millie and Jenny they both looked sun tanned and happy.

"Good time ladies?"

"Really enjoyed it Daniel. I think we both needed it, didn't we Millie?"

"We certainly did Jenny. Daniel dropped Jenny off at Ringo's in Liverpool, then they set off for London.

"So, what have you been up to Daniel, behaving I hope?"

"I have been to Scotland, well Paisley."

Millie looked shocked because she knew that meant it was the diaries that had taken him there. Daniel decided to say that yes it had been the diaries, but he hadn't done anything and had met Lee–Anne who he was now going to live with.

"Isn't it a bit soon Daniel? Sorry love I am only thinking of you, and you do seem very happy, and might I say a bit tidier. She must be good for you this Lee-Anne," and Millie smiled.

"When are you moving up there?"

"Tomorrow."

"Oh, wow that soon. Well I will come and visit you, and you make sure you phone me at least once a week."

"Of course I will Aunty Millie and once we are settled you can come and stay. You will like Paisley."

"Well that would be lovely Daniel."

It was 10.30pm when Daniel dropped Millie and her case off and he parked his car outside the house and went in. Daniel was feeling tired so brushed his teeth and dived into bed.

Dream number three came very quickly. The dream had Daniel as an infantry man in World War One. The dream started in Harry Skill's village of Brough. Harry was an apprentice Blacksmith aged fourteen in 1912. His master was Henry Dungdight, a huge man who at the village wakes would take bets on who could lift his anvil above their head for one minute. Nobody could beat Henry, although many tried.

The work was hard and very hot so when war broke out on August 4th 1914 Harry could see a way out. He was now a strong young man sixteen years old, and the thought of going abroad seemed exciting to young Harry. Harry joined up with two of his best pals Arthur Marsden and James Mellor. The government had decided to try and get men from the same villagers into the same regiments, mainly for companionship. The day arrived and Harry kissed his mum and told her not to worry that he would be back in a few weeks. Harry joined the line of soldiers alongside his mates Arthur and James. He was lapping up the attention the young girls from the surrounding villagers as they marched down the cobbled streets, festooned with bunting to catch the train. It seemed like every village for miles around had turned out to wave the brave lads on their way. Harry noticed big Henry Dungdight in the crowd so he put his thumb up.

"Good luck Harry lad," and he threw him a pen knife. "It's for good luck lad," Henry shouted.

Once on the train, Harry had chance to study his present from Henry. It was a pen knife shape but much bigger than normal with an ivory handle. Because Harry didn't know what to expect from the war he decided Henry must have given it him to protect himself, so he positioned it on the side of his ankle in his sock, out of sight but reachable if needed he thought.

GROVE

The journey to France seemed good. All the lads were in high spirits as they headed off to what they thought would be a few weeks abroad then back home. The reality was to be much different. Arthur Smith, James Elliot and Harry Skills were assigned to the First Battalion of the Sherwood Foresters.

It was 2.00am and Daniel woke from his dream which was odd because the other two dreams had come to some sort of conclusion, but this was cut short. Daniel lay tossing and turning until 8.30am when he decided that maybe he should get some packing done for the return to Paisley. The very first thing he did was to make sure the diaries he had from his grandfather and mother were safely packed. Daniel then set about his wardrobe. As he started to pack he realised what a mess he had been before going to Paisley. So he decided that he was going to give all the grunge clothes to a charity shop, and first thing he would do back in Paisley was to get a haircut and some new clothes. Daniel felt for the first time that his life somehow had a purpose. After losing his mother so cruelly before he got to know her, and not having any blood relatives, it had been left to Millie to bring him up, and she had found it very hard. Millie was a super surrogate mother but it just wasn't the same. He packed his clothes and took them down with his CD collection to the local charity shop. On leaving the shop Daniel felt liberated. He decided to get a coffee from Starbucks and sit for a few minutes next to a small lake. Daniel had almost finished his coffee when a man sat next to him. At first Daniel didn't take much notice. The man was wearing a bright orange jumper and it was then that Daniel realised who it was. He reeled back in shock as the man turned to him. It was Leviathan Harkan.

"Enjoying the sunshine Daniel?"

"What do you want?"

"How have you found me here?"

"I know every move you make Daniel, and at some time in the not so distant future all will be revealed."

"What the hell do you mean? Why are you following me? Keep away from me."

Harkan just ignored Daniel's protesting.

"I believe congratulations are in order are they not?"

"Look I don't know who you are or what you want from me."

By now Harkan was devouring a doughnut. The jam had spread in a disgusting way around his mouth and his longue tongue licked it making a weird noise.

"You disgust me, keep away," and Daniel got up and hurried away. From a safe distance he looked back, but nobody was sitting the bench.
Back at his house he told Millie that he had given all his clothes to the charity shop and he was getting his haircut. Millie seemed genuinely pleased at Daniel's revelation. Before he left for Paisley, Millie decided she needed to ask if Daniel had any dreams. Daniel knew if he had said yes Millie would have been upset, so he told a little white lie. Millie seemed contented with his answer and kissed him, pressing five hundred pounds into his hand.

"Have a safe journey and phone me when you get there."

"I will Aunty Millie, thank you for everything."

With tears rolling down Millie's face Daniel set off for Paisley. He was excited about his new life but also a little unsure about the dreams, Grove and Leviathan Harkan, and what had Harkan meant about congratulations were in order he thought.

It was almost 10.00pm when Daniel arrived at Lee-Anne's flat. He had phoned her to say he was an hour away. Lee-Anne was waiting for him looking excited. What bit of luggage he had he took into the house, then he kissed Lee-Anne.

"Wow the table looks lovely. What's the special occasion Lee-Anne?"

"Well the start of our new life together, and I have some other news. I have been sick in the morning so I thought I had a tummy bug, but not sure how you will take this, but I'm pregnant Daniel."

Daniel looked at Lee-Anne like he had seen a ghost.

"Pregnant?"

"Oh ugh, brilliant."

"Do you mean that Daniel?"

"Yes of course, it was just a bit of a shock."

Daniel kissed Lee-Anne to reassure her that everything was fine. It now made sense what Harkan said. But how the hell did he know? Daniel decided the next day, while Lee-Anne was at work, that he was going to Harkan's book shop to get the bottom of what his game was.

Daniel arrived at Brook Street. The book shop windows were covered in cobwebs and the maroon painted door had peeling paint. Daniel entered the shop and shouted, "Mr Harkan?"

Nobody came so he started looking at the books on the shelves. Suddenly Daniel could feel an eerie presence behind him, it was Harkan.

"I wondered what time you would arrive to see me."

"Look I am not playing games anymore. Who are you? How do you know so much about me, and how did you know Lee-Anne was pregnant?"

"My name is Leviathan."

Daniel took exception to this.

"Stop bloody playing around. What do you want from me?"

"Daniel, do not be so impatient. I told you all will be revealed."

"You think you are so clever don't you Harkan? So, tell me what do these dreams mean and why have I been brought to Paisley, and in particular Grove? Is this all to do with my ancestors?"

"That is for you to find out. Tea perhaps young Daniel?"

"You can stick your tea where the sun doesn't shine. Just stay away from me and Lee-Anne."

"I think you will find you came to me, Daniel," Harkan said as Daniel stormed out of the book shop.

It was lunchtime and Lee-Anne had said she would meet Daniel for lunch at the Green Tankard. He was feeling agitated as he entered the pub. Lee-Anne was already there and Murdo guessed who she was so introduced himself.

"Daniel what are you drinking?"

"I'm ok Murdo, thank you. Just going to sit in the corner with Lee-Anne and have a bite to eat."

"I envy you laddie she is a pretty wee lassie."

Lee-Anne coloured up and they sat in the window and ordered lunch.

"Are you ok Daniel? Where have you been this morning?"

"I'm fine Lee-Anne," he said but he knew he wasn't.

"I have been looking at books at the bookshop on Brook Street."

"Bookshop on Brook Street? There isn't one Daniel."

"Yes, there is opposite the plaque that tells you about them hanging people there back in the day."

"Think you are cracking up. I have never seen a book shop there."

"I bet you a fiver."

"Ok Daniel let's eat this and you can show me."

They finished their lunch and said goodbye to Murdo and headed for Brook Street. On the way he wished he hadn't said about it. The last thing he wanted was for Harkan to be about so there was no way he was going in. They arrived at the cobbled street and wandered down it. Lee-Anne was saying she would have a box of chocolates instead of the fiver. They finally arrived at the site of the book shop. To Daniel's horror there was no book shop. The shop was covered in cobwebs and boarded up

"There you go, chocolates please handsome," said Lee-Anne.

"I must have been on another street."

"There is a WH Smith on the High Street."

"Must have been that one," Daniel said trying to cover his tracks.

Daniel brought Lee-Anne her chocolates and dropped her back at work before making his way back to Brook Street. To his total amazement the book shop was there and Harkan was just leaving, so Daniel hid in a door way until he had gone. Daniel decided to go back to the flat and read his grandfather Liam's diary to see if there were any clues to all this.

It was 6.10pm when Lee-Anne came back from work. On entering the flat Daniel had fallen asleep and had dropped the diary on the floor. Lee-Anne bent down to pick it up and was intrigued so started reading it. She had been reading for about half an hour when Daniel woke up. He rubbed his eyes.

"Hi, you are early?"

"Yeah, I have been sick a couple of times. We weren't very busy so Margot said I could go early. When I came in you were fast asleep so I didn't bother you. You had dropped this diary, hope you don't mind I have read some of it. Whose is it?"

Now it was decision time. Did he tell Lee-Anne the story or lie to keep her protected? He loved her and didn't want to keep secrets as he thought that would be a bad way to start.

"Sit down Lee-Anne, I need to tell you everything."

"Oh Daniel, this sounds bad."

"Just bear with me. Liam Egan was my grandfather, although I never met him. Liam had dreams that appeared to take him to some kind of parallel universe. He was a slave from Ireland and was taken from his home and made to work the sugar cane the Caribbean. If you read the diaries, his

real life and his dream life entwined
so much. My grandma was a black
woman, very successful, and in his
diaries he had written about Shona
who was Cabhan's eventual wife, who
was also a black slave girl. I looked
up the name Shona and the equivalent
name in English is Joan which was
Liam's wife's name, and she was also
black."

"I am loving this Daniel."

"Now you have the basics, read the
diaries and all will become clear.
When you have read and understood
them I will tell you about my parents.
Well my parent, I never knew my
father. I'll make tea you sit and read
the diaries."

Daniel hadn't dreamt while he was
asleep so wasn't sure what would
happen tonight when he fell asleep,
but at least Lee-Anne would have
some kind of understanding about
everything.

It was almost 11.50pm when Lee-Anne completed the second diary.

"That's amazing Daniel but are you sure they are not just his dreams, nothing to do with time travel or anything like that?"

"You will see what I mean when you read Mum's diaries and then mine."

"Look, let's call it a night. It's been a long day. Can I read your Mum's diaries in the morning? I'm not on shift until 3.00pm tomorrow?"

"If you want to, its best you know everything."

"I found your grandfather's diaries riveting."

Daniel waited for the next line that he thought Lee-Anne would ask, which he thought would be did he dream? The question wasn't forthcoming.

Murdo had texted Daniel to say could he come and start at the Green

Tankard the following day on the 3.00pm to finish shift.

"Best get off to bed Lee-Anne. That was Murdo, they want me in at 9.00am for a couple of hours to show me the ropes. Then I am on from 3.00pm until it closes."

"Ok sweetheart, let's get some shut eye."

The following morning Daniel left his mother's diaries on the coffee table with a note for Lee-Anne who he had left fast asleep in bed.

The Green Tankard was your typical city centre pub with three rooms. One would have been a smoke room before it was banned. One was what they would have called the lounge where men would bring their wives on a Saturday night, and the other room had the dartboard and pool table in it. Daniel was introduced to Amy Mosh, a Polish girl who acted as the manager. Amy was a small girl with long hair tied back in a pony-tail. She seemed very friendly, as did the lads in the kitchen. By the time Daniel had been shown everything it was almost 12.30pm and the pub was quite busy so he offered to work through. Amy said that would be great and it helped Daniel for when he was on his own at 3.00pm. He quickly let Lee-Anne know so she wouldn't be worried. She seemed fine with it she said she was engrossed in Jane Egan's diaries.

By the end of Amy Mosh's shift Daniel felt reasonably confident he could handle the bar, and of course Murdo was sat at the end of the bar for support. Well that's what Murdo called as he downed his third whisky. About 7.00pm the bar went quiet. The rush was over so Daniel had chance to talk to Murdo. He thought he would see if his friend knew anything about Brook Street.

"Had a wander down Brook Street today Murdo."

"Ya like the weird places Daniel?"

"What do you mean?"

"It's just legend round here."

"Go on then tell me."

"Well they used to hang people in that little square at the bottom of Brook Street, so folks say it's haunted. There used to be a few shops down there but all the owners died in strange circumstances."

"What like?"

"Well I can only just remember the people as I was only a wee bairn then. Angus Lockrie was the butcher and he said he had seen things in the street. He liked a wee dram so nobody took much notice. One day Catherine Scholes a local teacher called for her meat for the weekend and she found poor Angus with no head, but she said he was still walking about. Catherine screamed and she said Angus fell to the floor. Police could not verify her story and they just assumed she was in shock. The butchers closed when business declined because of the story told by Catherine Scholes."

"Some ten years later it reopened and it was a flower shop. The Council threw some money at it and the darkened street was tidied up. The proprietor was a young lassie called Tansy Roberts. At first the shop did well then one night Tansy said she had seen a portly figure of a man with no head. It was the worst thing she could say, business nose-dived. Tansy was almost bankrupt and had mentioned to one of her very few customers that she may have to close if things didn't pick up. Andrew Neely the local milkman was dropping a pint of milk on the door step of the flower shop and he thought

he saw Tansy. He wanted his bill
paying so he opened the door and to
his horror Tansy was there but with
no head. He said she had a bunch of
lilacs in her hand. Andrew shouted for
help and he said immediately Tansy's
body dropped to the floor."

"Were there anymore incidents?"

"No but you won't find anybody
my age down there laddie."

"Where was the shop?"

"It was opposite the plaque that
tells you about the hangings. It's been
empty for years and years. You can
tell which one. It's painted maroon
which was the last colour of the
flower shop."

"That was really interesting
Murdo."

"I guess that's worth a pint of
heavy and a Dewey hey lad?"

"I guess so Murdo."

Daniel's shift went ok. He had a
slight problem with a lager barrel but

Murdo sorted him out and of course that cost a large Dewey.

Daniel arrived back at Lee-Anne's flat where she had cooked him some tea. Although Daniel wasn't really hungry but he thought it best to eat it. It was 12.05am when they got into bed. Lee-Anne had the following day off but Daniel was due at the Green Tankard for 11.00am until 8.00pm. Daniel was soon fast asleep. He was back in Harry Skill's world.

Harry and his two mates had been assigned to some trenches near Grubon in France. This was nothing like he expected. The trenches smelt, they were up to their ankles in mud and rats ran everywhere.

"So much for a bloody holiday Harry?"

"Yeah, not quite what I was expecting Arthur."

"It will only be for a couple of week lads," said James.

"Hope you are right old mate, not sure I can stick this dump for a lot longer."

The Germans were bombarding No-Man's land with heavy artillery. Most days the whistle would go and the men were told to go over the top to try and make some ground on the Germans. The Captain seemed to be selective, not everybody had to go. James, Arthur and Harry soon realised once you went over the top chances of you getting back alive or in one piece were pretty slim. It was August 18th 1915. Harry's regiment had been told they were to go on the whistle. The previous day Captain Taylor had shot two lads who refused. The poor men had been over twice and only just got back. They were clearly scared but Taylor had no hesitation in shooting them. Harry and his mates knew then that the choice was not available.

First over was Arthur Marsden followed by two others then Harry then James. Harry and James could see Arthur he had gone about twenty yards when a shell hit him. Bits of poor Arthur flew everywhere. James was physically sick. The whistle went again and they rushed back dodging bullets and all other things that would kill them.

Out of three hundred men when Captain Taylor counted them back there were only twenty seven.

"You were wrong Harry, this ain't no bloody holiday. We will be next."

Captain Taylor was walking past and overheard James.

"Mellor, think yourself lucky lad. Twenty seven back is a result. Your regiment is being moved to Northern France to help with the push up there.

Get your things together and go and fight for your country."

The arrogance from Taylor struck a bad chord with James Mellor. His best mate had just been blown to pieces and this idiot was talking about fighting for his country. James couldn't hold himself. He hit Taylor with everything he had. The Captain fell back and the other Privates held James back. The Captain told Harry's regiment to ship out but Mellor would not be going with them. Harry felt bad but he couldn't do anything.

Three months went by and Harry wasn't in the trenches. He found himself in Lasonel, a small town on the French German border. They had been fighting for three days when Harry's regiment managed to take the town. Harry hated this war and the killing, but he was a fair man. Harry stumbled on a barn where he found a German soldier in a corner under some hay. The man looked petrified. He had a cut to his leg and he wasn't armed. Harry pointed his rifle at him and the man begged for his life. Harry suddenly came to his senses and looked at the small dark-haired man shaking with the fear he was about to shoot.

"What's your name, private?"

The man only just understood. He said, "Alois Schicklgruber."

Harry lifted his gun and left him where he was. As he walked away he felt good inside. At least this bloody war hadn't taken his belief in mankind he thought.

Daniel woke. Lee-Anne was rocking him.

"Daniel it's almost 10.30am. You have work in half an hour."

"Oh crap," he rushed round. As he was about to leave he kissed Lee-Anne, but then she said something to him.

"You were dreaming again last night. Who was Arthur and James, Daniel?"

"I'll explain when I get back. I need to do my diary. Love you," and he left for the Green Tankard.
The Green Tankard was empty when he arrived so Daniel bottled up and wiped the shelves. It was 1.00pm and still no sign of Murdo and still nobody in the bar. Daniel came up from stacking the crisps behind the bar to see Leviathan Harkan standing at the bar. He was dressed in his usual weird way with a green shirt, a blue jacket and maroon trousers.

"Good afternoon Daniel."

"What do you want?"

"That isn't very polite of you young Mr Egan. I will have a small cider."

"No, I meant what do you want?" Daniel said again.

"A drink young man. That is your job to serve customers, am I correct?"

"What is with your bookshop? How the hell do you make it change back into a derelict shop?"

"Not sure I know what you are talking about Daniel. How is your girlfriend and that future baby of yours?"

"How do you know about that?"

"What about your dreams, are you finding them interesting?"

Just then Billy the owner shouted, "Daniel. Seeing that we are quiet would you mind doing some food preparation?"

"No not a problem. I just have one customer at the moment."

"Where?"

Daniel turned around there was no sign of Leviathan Harkan. This man is screwing with my head Daniel thought. Another two hours passed and Billy told Daniel he could leave the bar now as nobody was in if he wanted to call it a day. Daniel left for home. He didn't phone Lee-Anne he thought he would surprise her. He arrived home and found Lee-Anne in tears.

"Whatever is a matter sweetheart?"

"Some man came to the flat today. He was like weird a bit like a Doctor Who. I answered the door and he touched my tummy."

"What did he say?"

"He smiled at me and said baby eh? How would he know, I am hardly showing? He had this disgusting tongue and he licked round his lips as he was talking."

It was now time to tell Lee-Anne everything Daniel thought.

"Sit down Lee-Anne, I'll make us a coffee and explain as much as I know."

Daniel sat and went through everything Lee-Anne could relate to.

The stories of Daniel's grandad Liam, and his Mum. When he started his story Lee-Anne was shocked and then the real emotion kicked in.

"It all seems so weird Daniel. What does it all mean?"

"I honestly don't know sweetheart. I wasn't going to tell you all this, but now that Harkan has been here I am concerned."

"What about your dreams Daniel?"

"I can't make sense of any of them so far. They are not like Liam's and Mum's. They seemed to have an ending but mine are just random things in history."

"I think I should go and see Nicola Gielbert who Mum and Grandad saw, if Aunty Millie will sort for me."

"She was the lady that does the regression is that correct Daniel?"

"Yes, that is the lady. I am going to phone Aunty Millie. I'm not working this weekend so would be an ideal time."

"I'm coming with you Daniel. I'm not staying here with this creep about."

"I know sweetheart, let me phone Aunty Millie."

"Hello Daniel, thought you had forgotten your old Aunty Millie."

"Sorry I have had so much on. Can you do something for me? Could you book a session with Nicola Gielbert on Saturday? Me and Lee-Anne are coming down for the weekend."

"You are having the dreams, aren't you?"

"I will explain everything Aunty Millie."

"Ok love can't wait to see you and Lee-Anne."

"Can you pick us up from the train station. I think the train gets in about 9.00am."

"Of course I will. Let me ring Nicola and I will call you back Daniel."

About twenty minutes later Millie called back to say Nicola Gielbert was ok for Saturday.

"I am tempted to go and give Harkan a piece of my mind."

"I am coming as well. He has no right to come to where we live Daniel."

Lee-Anne and Daniel set off for Brook Street and the book shop. They made their way down the little cobbled street with its dim lighting like something out a Dickens novel. Eventually they got to the little square.

"Where is it Daniel?"

"There?"

"But that's all shut-up. I don't think it's been a shop for years. It's no different than when I won my bet?"

"It was here honestly Lee-Anne."

"Are you sure it wasn't one of your dreams?"

Daniel felt annoyed that Lee-Anne was making light of it all.

"If it wasn't a book shop where did Harkan come from?"

"Well you said you first met him in the hotel at breakfast. Maybe he got in your sub-conscious and that put him in your dream of the book shop?" Clearly Lee-Anne was convinced it was just a dream so Daniel decided to go along with it, but was determined to go back when he was on his own.

CHAPTER THREE

Saturday morning arrived and Daniel and Lee-Anne's train pulled into St Pancras station. Millie came running over and kissed Daniel.

"This is Lee-Anne, Aunty Millie."

"Hello Lee-Anne. I have heard lots about you."

"Hope it was all nice, Mrs Trench."

"Please call me Millie."

"What time am I seeing Nicola Gielbert?"

"4.00pm was the only slot she had got Daniel."

"That's fine, thank you for sorting for me. Let's grab a coffee and I will tell you the full story."

Daniel told Millie how he arrived in Paisley and had found St Matthews Church in a village three miles out of Paisley at a place called Grove. He explained how he arrived at the church and a little old lady appeared from nowhere and gave him a key and instructions, and she had said she was the keeper of the key. He also explained how she disappeared as quickly as she arrived.

Millie was shocked, the prophecy previously that she had been told was coming to life. Nicola Gielbert had said after a session with Liam's mum Jane, that Harold Litton, a kind of soothsayer, had said a boy would be born who would then carry the burden of mankind.

At precisely 4.00pm they rang Nicola Gielbert's door bell.

"Do come in," she said.

Gielbert was dressed immaculately in a brown dress with a small silver cross hanging round her neck and brown and cream shoes which complimented her dress perfectly.

"So, Daniel isn't it?"

"Yes, that's correct."

"I need to run through a few things before we have the session and you will need to sign the forms. It's basically my insurance policy to say you fully understand what you are undertaking."

Daniel read the forms then signed and dated them. Nicola put on some soothing music and asked Lee-Anne and Millie to sit on the couch and to be perfectly quiet. Then Nicola started her work.

"Where are you Daniel?"

At first Daniel didn't react.

"We are her to help you Daniel. What is troubling you?"

Daniel replied, but in a deep throaty voice, that he wasn't troubled and that everyone else is. Nicola then asked Daniel what year it was. Again he didn't answer at first but then suddenly he grabbed the cross and chain from Nicola's neck and threw it across the room. By now Daniel was foaming at the mouth like a rabid dog. He was thrashing first left then right and he was kicking out at imaginary things. Nicola was desperately trying to bring him round. Eventually Daniel reacted and calmed down before finally opening his eyes. Nicola Gielbert's neck was red where he had yanked the cross and chain but Daniel didn't seem in any distress.

"What happened said Daniel?"

"You appeared to have a bad reaction to regression Daniel."

Daniel realised something was wrong Lee-Anne had been crying and Nicola's neck was in a real state.

"I need to know Miss Gielbert, what happened?"

Let me make us a coffee and I will discuss my findings. Gielbert arrived back with a tray of coffee and some speciality biscuits.

"It is my professional opinion, for what it's worth Daniel, that in some way you are being possessed. I have never seen anybody react like that in my practise. Both your grandfather and your Mum were very special cases for regression, the likes of which I don't think I will ever see in my lifetime again. The difference is you most likely had a fit, which means for me it isn't good to be giving you anymore regression sessions."

"What do you mean?"

"I don't think it's safe for me. Your reaction to me I think has something to do with my sessions with your mother and grandfather. Something stirred inside you."

"You have to help me Miss Gielbert please."

"Look, I have a Catholic priest who is a friend. I would like him to be present if you wish another session."

"Can we do it tomorrow, as I live in Scotland now?"

"Let me phone Father Hegarty."

Nicola went in the other room and when she came back she confirmed 2.00pm on Sunday. Daniel felt a little down as they sat sipping coffee in Covent Garden.

"Look love, we don't have to do this."

"We do Aunty Millie. I need to know why me and my family have been subjected to this awful burden."

I wish Jamie was here Millie thought. Daniel noticed that Millie had to hold her coffee with both hands.

"I thought you were sorted Aunty Millie?

"I was Daniel, but it came back a few days ago." Millie kept her concern. She too had a terrible nightmare which she didn't want to share with Daniel. Daniel excused himself from the table to go to the toilet.

"Will Daniel be alright Millie? I am worried, we have this baby on the way."

"Look Lee-Anne, something has troubled the Egan family since Liam and the Ouija board session all those years ago, and in my opinion if we don't sort Daniel out it will consume him, and your hope of any happiness."

"What's wrong?" Daniel said as he arrived back.

"Oh nothing, I was just asking your Aunty Millie about the shaking problem."

"Thought you might be saying what a delectable, good looking man you have the pleasure to be with."

"Get you bighead," said Lee-Anne and they both laughed.

The following day at Millie's there was a knock on the door and an elderly man dressed in full church robes was at Millie's flat door.

"Father Hegarty?"

"That's correct, you must be Mrs Trench."

"Please come in Father. This is Daniel and his partner Lee-Anne."

"I see you are with child my dear?"

"Yes Father, six months gone."

"Then we need to sort Daniel out."

Millie made tea for everyone and they sat at the kitchen table while Father Hegarty explained all about evil spirits.

"I tend to call evil spirits stray spirits. Spiritual possession, if indeed this is what Daniel has, can be the cause of mental illness. Medical opinion through the ages think science has been sceptical of its existence, yet it is quite a common occurrence. The only way to counter this phenomenon in my experience is with accurate spiritual knowledge. You need to tell me everything you know. Everything since this began has been documented; first with Liam Egan Daniel's Grandad and then his mother Jane Egan."

Daniel produced the diaries.

"I need to read these thoroughly, then I will need you to tell me line for line how this as affected you Daniel. This may take a good few hours so if you have things to do please don't let me hold you up."

Daniel and Lee-Anne decided to go for a walk and Millie said she had some ironing. They left this little old man with white hair and goatee beard reading the diaries. Every now and again Millie would check on him and make another tea. On one of these occasions Father Hegarty looked at Millie quite strangely.

"How long have your hands shook like this Mrs Trench?"

"My left hand about six months, but it stopped recently but now both shake again."

"I don't want to concern you, but it's my experience that you may have also been consumed by this spirit, but your goodness is fighting it."

Millie looked shocked.

"I see that you are a caring lady which is working in your favour, but unless you believe this the spirit will consume you also."

"This isn't about me Father."

"I'm afraid it is though Mrs Trench. I would like to try and contact this spirit in you also. I am guessing that you have had this shaking looked at medically but they are baffled, correct?"

"Well they need more tests Father."

"That is a medical way of politely saying they are baffled."

It took the Father the rest of the afternoon to complete reading the diaries and Daniel and Lee-Anne were back from their walk. Father Hegarty asked that he and Daniel speak alone while Daniel told his story. Daniel missed out the bit about the disappearing book shop for fear of ridicule. Eventually Daniel was laid on Millie's king size bed for the exorcism.

"You all have to be aware that a stray spirit can be very aggressive. It might be wise Lee-Anne to step out of the room, with you being with child." Father Hegarty started the exorcism. This lasted for almost an hour but to his and Millie's surprise absolutely nothing happened.

"It appears that no wandering soul is present within you Daniel. How do you feel Daniel?"

"To be honest Aunty Millie I have a weird feeling but like a good feeling."

"Mrs Trench do you want me to look at you?"

"Thank you Father Hegarty but I think I will be fine. I think I may have the start of Parkinson's disease not any stray soul possessing me but thank you."

Father Hegarty could sense Millie's mistrust but decided to let sleeping dogs lie.

The following morning Daniel and Lee-Anne decided to go into London to do some last-minute shopping before the return journey to Paisley. It was a lovely summer's day and everything seemed so good Daniel thought as he held Lee-Anne's hand to cross the road. Suddenly Lee-Anne doubled up in pain.

"You ok?"

She could hardly speak. Daniel flagged down a taxi.

"Take me to the nearest hospital please mate," he said to the taxi driver. The driver didn't turn round but nodded. Daniel was too concerned for Lee-Anne to care at the man's ignorance. They arrived ten minutes later and Daniel helped Lee–Anne out of the taxi and fumbled in his pocket handing the taxi driver his change. The man pushed back his cap he was wearing and said, "Good luck." Suddenly Daniel realised it was Harkan. The taxi drew away. What the hell is happening he thought?

Three hours passed before a doctor pulled Daniel aside.

"I am sorry to say Lee-Anne has lost the baby Daniel."

Daniel didn't want to cry in front of Lee-Anne as he could see the hurt she was going through. Then Daniel's mind started racing. Did Harkan have anything to do with this or was it just coincidence? Why was he driving a taxi and of all the taxi's in London did he be the one to pick them up? Daniel decided it was time he and Harkan had some serious words. He never told Lee-Anne about the taxi ride.

The first chance he had once back in Paisley he went to the book shop. Of course it was still the same as last time he visited, crumbling paint work and no sign of Harkan. Days became weeks followed by months. The dreams had stopped and they had tried for another baby but to no avail. Millie sadly wasn't getting much better, her shakes were sometime ok and other times uncontrollable. Daniel thought about moving back to London to look after her but Lee-Anne didn't want to leave Paisley. So Daniel would go down periodically to check on his Aunty Millie and she was always the same, cheerful and pleased to see him.

It was on the third anniversary of Daniel coming to Paisley that he decided to go back to the Church and to Grove. Lee-Anne had gone for a long weekend with some friends to a health Spa so he was at a loose end. Daniel arrived at the Church, he opened the old Church door and went inside. To Daniel's surprise although he had to unlock the door, the little old lady he had spoken to on the first day was sitting in the pew at the front with her hands clasped praying. Daniel very quietly walked down the aisle and sat next to her. She seemed to be in some kind of a trance. He could feel his heart thumping, it felt like he could jump out of his chest at any time. Eventually she stopped what she was doing and looked at Daniel.

"They said you would come today. You are in grave danger."

"Who are you? How did you get in Church? It was locked, I opened it with the key you gave me. Why am I in grave danger?"

The old lady turned to him. The left-hand side of her face was swollen and he could see two marks in the centre of the swelling as if somebody had got a magic marker and put two dots on the swelling.

"Tell me what the danger is?"

"It is all around you and when it comes you won't expect it. Only you, the chosen one, can save humanity," and with that she just disappeared. Daniel felt nervous but decided he would head into Grove so he walked down the aisle. There was no sign of the lady with the swollen face and the two marks. Daniel locked the big old church door.

GROVE

Once outside it had turned quite cool.
There was a light breeze and it was
heading toward dusk. Daniel decided
to try and find his ancestor's cottage.
Grove was such an eerie place, the
cottages that were left had seen much
better days. As he wandered down
almost to the bottom of the village
there was an old wooden bench.
Daniel sat on the bench contemplating
what to do next. Daniel hadn't been
fazed by the old lady disappearing,
just intrigued at all this skulduggery.
He had been sitting there for almost
ten minutes thinking, when from out
of the shadows of the woods behind
appeared a man. He came and sat next
to Daniel. The man wasn't dressed in
the current era. He was in what could
only be described as sack cloth. He
was unshaven and he had just one
tooth when he smiled at Daniel.

"Good evening Daniel."
"Do I know you?"

"You will have heard of me."

"Who are you?"

"Let's save that until later. I am pleased we have finally met I have been waiting for this day for so long. Come with me I have something to show you."

Daniel wasn't sure to go with this man but he wondered if it might help to understand what the hell was going on.

Daniel and the man walked into the forest which appeared overgrown but as they walked the overgrown bramble covering the floor seemed to part to make a clean path. Daniel thought they had walked about a mile.

"Right young Daniel, we are nearly here. You see that oak tree with a cut out in it. Just walk in there and I will follow."

Daniel did as he was told. As he entered the oak tree it was like he had been put in a food blender. Everything became jumbled up and he found himself on the village green of Grove, not now, but in the past. People were busy rushing about, kids were playing in the dusty street, chickens were scavenging for worms. He was half expecting Robin Hood to appear. Seconds after arriving, the man arrived.

"Who are you? Where am I?"

"You are in Grove Daniel before evil came to this town. Follow me."

The man took Daniel down a side street before arriving at a small cottage.

"This is my wife Mary and my daughter Allop. Allop is poorly that is why I have brought you here."

"What year is this Mr?"

"The year of our Lord 1496 Daniel."

"What is your name."

"My name is Arthur Skilling."

"Why have you brought me here?"

"Because you are to save humanity as my wife told you at the church."

"That was your wife Mr Skilling, with the swollen face, who gave me the key to the church and who I saw today in the church."

"Aye that be Mary."

Daniel looked at Mary Skilling and she was a beautiful woman.

"What is wrong with your daughter?"

"She has the fever and will die Daniel."

"I am sorry but what use am I to you?"

"You need to see the evil that Egan brought to this once thriving community."

"Am I dreaming Mr Skilling?"

"Maybe you are, maybe you are not, but whichever way soon you will see evil young Daniel."

Skilling and the family had a bed made up for Daniel and he slept.

There was no dreaming and he slept well.

The following day Arthur Skilling said Daniel had been with them a few months and it was now January 1497 and the winter was harsh. By February it was so cold and the dead were piling up in the street dead from starvation and cold. One man who he saw every day was a colossus of a man Skilling said that was Dermot Egan. Daniel could see how the villagers appeared frightened of his ancestor.

"You Daniel must kill Egan," said Skilling.

"What kill my great whatever grandparent? I don't think so Mr Skilling. If you have brought me here for that you have wasted your time. Daniel stayed all through the harsh winter. Skilling kept badgering him to kill Dermot Egan or he would not let him go back.

"All you have been through could be wiped from time if you kill this evil man. Think of the lives you are saving."

Daniel was still adamant he would not kill his ancestor.

"Why don't you do it Mr Skilling?"

"Because I am not a murderer, but you are."

Some weeks passed and Skilling's daughter died. Before dying she vomited a yellow bile. Mr and Mrs Skilling were convinced this was some kind of evil spirit leaving the poor girl's body. Daniel decided he needed to somehow get back. So, on a very cold morning he headed into the woods he finally found the oak tree and sat in the hollow. Nothing happened he waited and waited at nightfall Skilling arrived.

"You stupid boy. You don't go back unless I say. My wife told you that first day when she gave you the key to the church who you were but you don't take heed. You will go back but trust in my words your end will come and it will be catastrophic."

With the words ringing in his ears the feeling of being in a food blender happened and Daniel found himself outside the tree but back in his real time.
How was he going to explain this to anyone he thought? Daniel headed home convinced that at least five or six months had passed. Daniel opened the door to go inside and see Lee-Anne.

"Hello," he shouted.

"Daniel we are up here, we have had such a lovely day. Come and have a drink of Prosecco with me and the girls."

Daniel was shocked. He had been in Grove with Skilling at least five months yet it had only been a day in the real world. Daniel began to question his sanity. He decided to leave the girls and fill in his diary with the events. He could hear the girls giggling and laughing as he fell asleep.

The following morning he explained to Lee-Anne what had happened and while she said she believed him Daniel could sense some scepticism in her voice. Daniel had work the next day and now that he was General Manager at the Green Tankard he liked to go in a bit earlier to ensure everything was right. Invariably this often meant cleaning behind the bar and stocking the shelves while Murdo sat drinking and talking to him. He had never shared the stories about his family with Murdo but something kept telling him he should.

"What are you doing at 3.00pm when I finish Murdo?"

"Probably still here, why?"

"Wondered if I could have a chat with you?"

"Oh, lassie trouble hey laddie?"

"No, not at all, just something I would like to tell you."

"Ok, look forward to it, but if I have to be a listener then a large Dewey would help."

"You bloody old scoundrel," Daniel said as he gave Murdo the large Dewey on the house.
With his shift finished Daniel poured himself a drink and a large Dewey for Murdo and they sat in the corner so that they wouldn't be disturbed.

"So laddie what's this all about?"

"It's going to sound farcical but trust me all this happens. I will start back to front. I am not up here doing my family tree."

"Never thought you were laddie."

"Really Murdo, am I that transparent?"

"No not really, but there have been others before you in my lifetime and my Grandad told me stories from his lifetime. You are looking for answers, aren't you?"

"Yes, I am Murdo, I never knew my grandparents but I have their diaries. My Grandad was Liam Egan who lived in Ireland as a man called Cabhan. It was just after the Cadiz war. Pirates came to his village knowing most men-folk had not returned from the war, so they knew there were rich pickings."
Poor Cabhan was only about fourteen and he was taken to Barbados as a white slave, they didn't call them that, but that's what they were. My Grandad Liam Egan wrote everything down in a diary. It all started in London where he lived. He was a trader and on his birthday his friends took him out to celebrate. They eventually ended up at one of the

friend's house and a game Ouija was suggested."

"That's nasty stuff to play with Daniel."

"I agree Murdo, my Grand-father didn't want to play it but couldn't refuse being his birthday. Apparently so the diaries say, nobody got picked other than Liam and a name was spelt out. This name was Cabhan. My Grandad dreamt for many years and he documented everything. Eventually he met my Grandma Joan and in his dreams the slave girl he married was called Shona. I looked up the name and Joan means Shona in Barbados so it appeared these were not just coincidences. The dreams affected my Grandad severely and for many years he was in something of a coma. Joan was pregnant with my mother Jane so it was many years before he saw or even knew he had a daughter. They both died leaving Jane an orphan.

Aunty Millie and Uncle Jamie looked after her. They are not really Aunty and Uncle but Liam and Joan's best friends.
Eventually my mum went to Liverpool University, and that move was as if it was also planned like my life appears to be. In Liverpool she happened to call at a café which was run by a Jewish woman and her son. The Jewish woman was very old and had been through the holocaust. My mother's diaries show she was also inflicted with the same torment. During her dreams she is part of the holocaust and just like her dad she ended up in a coma. She eventually died but she had documented everything in the diaries."

"Murdo sat listening impassively to Daniel.

"Now it comes to me and my story which you will think I am nuts."

"Not at all, I am finding it very intriguing."

"Well in my mother's diaries I was told there was a place called Paisley and a little village called Grove. I was told to go to a church there and behind a picture of St John the Baptist there would be a safe. I had to enter some numbers, then there was another door which I had a key to open. Inside were two old scrolls. I have only managed to decipher one which said 'Now you have been chosen to end the world's misery. Be sure when you leave this place that you follow the manuscript in its entirety your path has been chosen.'"

"Daniel can I ask you? Do you use drugs?"

"Look Murdo I did dabble, but only marijuana and not for a long time."

"Look, let me borrow the diaries of Liam Egan and your mother and I might understand better."

"Oh, I'm not sure Murdo."

"Do you nay trust me laddie."

"Of course I do, but they are precious to me."

"Look I will have them read in a couple of days, then we can work on yours. What do you say laddie?"

"Ok then." Daniel always kept the diaries with him, he kind of felt safe being with them. He handed them over but kept his diary.

"Right I'm off for some tea, I will see you tomorrow Daniel."

"Ok Murdo."

Murdo walked away with the diaries.

CHAPTER FOUR

Three months had passed and Murdo had not been in the Green Tankard and Daniel was getting worried so he waited for Billy, the owner, to ask him where Murdo lived. Billy looked at Daniel in a totally bemused way.

"Murdo?"

"You know your mate Murdo that got me this job."

"I'm sorry Daniel. I don't know a Murdo. A woman rang up on your behalf said you were looking for work. I don't have any friends called Murdo? Look I best get on, I have my tax return to do."

Billy left Daniel standing in amazement. Who the hell was Murdo, and where were his diaries?

Months went by and Daniel had no more dreams. Murdo hadn't resurfaced and Daniel had asked Lee-

Anne to marry him. He phoned Millie, and of course, she was over the moon. Daniel invited her up for the wedding and said he would pick her up from the train station. Millie could not believe her eyes, the Daniel she saw he was well dressed with a proper haircut, as she called it, and dressed casually but smart. Lee-Anne had done a good job on him Millie thought.

The wedding was to be a grand affair at the Simmon Hotel near Paisley. Daniel had asked an old friend Jack Holgarth from London to be his best man. Luckily for Daniel, Jack had also smartened himself up and was a car salesman in Peckham, so he looked the part. Lee-Anne had two work mates as bridesmaids. The total wedding party was thirty six.

"Looking forward to meeting Lee-Anne's family, Daniel."

"Slight problem there, she doesn't have any Aunty Millie."

"What, no immediate family, and no Aunties and Uncles."

"She says not, and don't mention it she gets touchy about it."

"Oh, I won't Daniel, we can't say much with just me here can we?"

"Can't think of anybody better Aunty Millie."

"Aww thank you Daniel."

"We are going straight to church if that's ok Aunty Millie."

"I suppose so, do I look ok?"

Both of Millie's hands were shaking quite badly. Millie noticed Daniel looking.

"I know sweetheart, they don't know what it is. They have done loads of tests. They say it is possibly stress, so I retired from work and it's no better but there are a lot worse off Daniel," and she smiled.

Millie was always positive. Daniel decided to tell Millie about Murdo and the diaries and the time travel to Grove.

"This is all very weird Daniel. Are you still having dreams, be honest with me?"

"No Aunty Millie they seem to have stopped."

"Well at least that is something." She tugged on Daniel's lapel of his suit.

"Your Mum, Grandad and Grandma would have been so proud of you Daniel, all grown up and getting married."

Daniel just smiled at Millie, she had been such a good surrogate parent to him. The village church in Scolby was the chosen venue for the marriage. The church was a small Saxon church called St Helen's and it stood in about an acre of graveyards.

Daniel and Millie arrived and were met by Daniel's best man.

"Come on you two or Lee-Anne will be here before you are seated."

Jack, Daniel and Millie entered the church. The congregation was a mixture of Daniel's friends from The Green Tankard and Lee-Anne's from the hotel. They all turned and smiled. Almost ten minutes later Lee-Anne arrived. She had chosen a black wedding dress which Daniel knew would surprise everyone, Millie included, but it's what she wanted and it's her big day Daniel thought. Sure enough the wedding march played and Daniel could hear a little gasp from the congregation as Lee-Anne and the night porter Richie Thompson walked down the aisle. The ceremony began but a shock was about to happen when at the point where the vicar said, "If any man or women has any lawful reason why these two should not be married, speak now, or forever hold your peace."

Not a word was uttered from the congregation.

Just has the vicar was about to carry on, Jack the best man fell forward holding his throat. Richie Thompson rushed to his aid but he also then fell forward clutching his throat. The service stopped, there was pandemonium. People were trying to get a signal on their mobile phones, but the church seemed to be a dead spot. Daniel rushed outside to try and get a signal. Standing by an old gravestone was Harkan. He was dressed in all red, with blue shoes he smiled and waved.

Daniel started to walk over to him but he just disappeared into thin air. As Harkan disappeared suddenly Daniel had a signal. He called the emergency services and ran back in the church to see if he could help. It had got worse another seven people lay dying in the aisle. Daniel looked for Millie, she gestured she was ok. Lee-Anne took Daniel to one side and said she didn't want to get married. The day was ruined and it was a sign. Although Daniel was upset with Lee-Anne he could understand. When all the victims had been taken to hospital they decided to still have the meal and the night entertainment as it had been paid for.

Approaching 10.30pm Daniel phoned Paisley hospital to see how Jack was. It was then that the news hit him like a thunderbolt. All nine victims had died, and they all had the same injuries which looked like a snake bite to the neck.

Daniel's blood ran cold, having seen Harkan outside, and the old lady with what looked like a snake bite on her swollen face, what the hell was this all about? Daniel was in bits. He had to call Jack's parents who he had known since he was a little boy and tell them Jack was dead. How could he live with himself knowing this had something to do with what was happening in his life?

Two days later Daniel decided to go and see Ewan Hufton again to see if he could throw any light on this. He didn't tell Lee-Anne. She didn't seem to care about the dead people and never mentioned the wedding. It seemed she was oblivious to what had happened.

Daniel had taken Millie that morning for her train back to London. After dropping her off he headed to Cragmouth in Colley Road, Paisley. Daniel arrived at about 3.00pm. He could see Professor Hufton's grey Subaru on the drive so he knocked on the door. As he did the door burst open. Assuming he hadn't shut it correctly Daniel shouted, "Hello."

He could hear a muffled sound so decided to enter the house. To his horror Hufton was laying on the kitchen floor. Daubed on the walls in what looked like blood it said 'Reinará' across all four walls. Daniel was trying to attend to poor Ewan Hufton. Blood was pumping out of a neck wound. Ewan suddenly heard sirens, either ambulance or police, he wasn't sure. He heard somebody say, "That's him."

Police swarmed the kitchen and dragged Daniel away from Hufton who had just said to Daniel, "Evil."

"What are you doing, I am trying to help him?"

Daniel was handcuffed and marched outside into a waiting police car. A woman in her mid fifties kept pointing at him strangely. Daniel was taken to the police station where he was put in a room and two detectives started questioning.

"What's your name?"

"Daniel Egan."

"Why were you robbing Mr Hufton?" said one of the surly detectives.

"I wasn't robbing him, I found him like he was."

"Come on son, why not make this easy on yourself? We have a witness that said you broke into the house. You have blood all over you. We find you over a bleeding body, and to add to this, the witness told our constable that Mr Hufton had told her that you had been hassling him before in a menacing manner. We have you bang to rights laddie."

"I want a lawyer."

"Really laddie, I think Mr Hufton would have wanted a life until you took it."

"I came to see him about some books he had written."

"Have you ever used drugs laddie, and be careful we can check your answer."

"Yes, but only when I was a stupid teenager and only marijuana."

"So, you think by your statement that using drugs is no big deal laddie?"

"I never said that I just answered your question."

"I think we have a smart arse on our hands here sergeant," the surly detective said to his colleague.

"Ok, lock him up. Arrange for a solicitor for him for tomorrow and allow him one telephone call."

Daniel was in shock. He phoned Lee-Anne telling her what happened and he asked her to phone Aunty Millie. The following day Millie had arranged for Michael Glick a top London lawyer to fly to Paisley to represent Daniel. Millie and Lee-Anne sat waiting while Glick and Daniel entered the interview room. The tape was set running and the two detectives introduced themselves.

"Ok Daniel, we have insurmountable evidence that you murdered Mr Hufton. The kitchen knife has your DNA all over it. We have found no other DNA on the murder weapon. Your DNA was also found on the body. We have a witness who states Mr Hufton had told her that he feared you."

"Gentlemen, my client found the door of Mr Hufton's house open, he went to help the man, not murder him. Your inference with regard to DNA, of course his DNA would be evident, why would the killer leave their DNA? My client had visited Mr Hufton on a previous occasion to talk with him about Grove, a village near Paisley. He had written books about a place my client was researching for his family tree."

"Do you know Mr Glick, I am of the mind you may be correct? My little niggle in this is why Mr Hufton felt threatened enough to tell his neighbour of his concern? Daniel, would you have any thoughts on this?"

"I found Mr Hufton a bit of strange man. He was quite welcoming at first but didn't particularly want to discuss Grove."

"Well Mr Egan we only deal in facts, not this hocus pocus mumbo jumbo people talk about the village of Grove. The fact is young man you were at the scene. I think I believe your story. We may need to speak again but you are free to go for now."

Daniel and Glick shook hands with the detectives and left the incident room Daniel thanked Glick.

"Come on let's go and celebrate," said Millie.

"I can't I have to work."

"Ok Lee-Anne, we will see you later."

Glick left for London with Millie's gratitude ringing in his ears.

"Come on Aunty Millie, let's go to the Argentinean restaurant, my treat."

They arrived at Gringo's a small family restaurant in the older part of Paisley. While the waiter fetched the drinks Millie was keen to ask Daniel about Lee-Anne.

"Are you two ok?"

"I'm not sure Aunty Millie. Since we lost the baby and then the wedding mess, it really hasn't been the same. In fact I have thought of coming home."

"If you are not happy Daniel then perhaps you should."

"Let's talk about this later after one of these fantastic steaks."

The food arrived.

"Blimey Daniel, not sure I can eat all this, it's massive."

"You won't get steak like this down London Aunty Millie."

The conversation turned to Professor Hufton.

"What happened Daniel?"

"I had decided to try and find out more. He had already warned me off last time. I don't think his murder was a robbery. I think whatever is stalking the Egan family will have to be addressed at some point. He had a shake like yours Aunty Millie."

"Maybe he had Parkinson's?"

"Is that what they say you have?"

"No Daniel they can't find anything, other than it might be a stress related thing."

"I feel like I am the end of the line for this evil thing affecting us, Aunty Millie."

"What do you mean by that son?"

"So much has happened since I have been here. Your shaking goes then comes back and the doctors can't find anything. Lee-Anne lost the baby after a visit from Harkan. The wedding and nine people died with what looked like snake bites. Arthur Skilling took me to Grove in 1496. I was there a good few months but in reality I was just out for a few hours. I gave Murdo the diaries. He was a good friend and got me the job, but I haven't seen him for four months. He has disappeared and when I ask people about him they say they don't know who I am talking about, Aunty Millie.

I have decided I am going to have a break from Lee-Anne and come back to London. I am going to move in with you and look after you."

"You don't have to do that Daniel."

"Aunty Millie, you have been everything to me since I was a little boy, and now it's your turn to be looked after."

Secretly Millie was over the moon, she could have Daniel all to herself. She had been so worried with all these evil things that had happened, and she felt he would be safer in London.

"If you are sure Daniel. I have a couple of contacts in the city, mates of Jamie, so I could probably get you a job trading like your Grandad used to do."

"Wow that would be awesome. I will take you for the train in the morning and then I will follow in a couple of days. I need tell Billy I am leaving and explain to Lee-Anne, that's if she is bothered."

"Oh, I am sure she is."

"Well don't say anything Aunty Millie I need to tell her."

"Of course, I won't say anything, that's your business."

The following morning Millie said goodbye to Lee-Anne, who to be honest wasn't over friendly anyway. Millie wondered if she was suffering with depression. She didn't say anything to Daniel for fear he might change his mind and not come to London. She knew she was being a bit selfish, but her shaking was getting worse. She was beginning to think there was something more seriously wrong with her than the doctors were saying.

At the station Millie kissed Daniel on the cheek and thanked him and told him how much she was looking forward to him coming to stay. Daniel waved her off and made his way back to Lee-Anne.

Daniel had fallen in love with Paisley and the people. Even though some of the things that had happened were weird and abnormal, he still liked it. Lee-Anne was a problem. Although they had fallen head over heels in love it now seemed like she didn't care for him anymore, so he needed to find out where he stood.

With woeful anticipation he entered the flat and called out to Lee-Anne. No reply came so he started looking round the house then he heard sobbing coming from the bedroom.

"Lee-Anne?"

She was sitting on the bed crying uncontrollably. Daniel sat next to her and put his arm's round her slim shoulders.

"Whatever is a matter?"

Lee-Anne started telling Daniel her story.

"The reason none of my family came to the wedding is they are locked up in Barlinnie prison Glasgow."

"What you have a mum and dad?"

"Yes, but I was too ashamed to tell you. They have been in there twenty years. I was four when I was put into care."

"What the hell did they do to be inside for so long?"

"Daniel, I have never spoken to anyone about this. I was born in Duloon which is a small fishing village on the West Coast of Scotland. You must understand I have very little memory of this, it is only what my social workers have told me. Apparently my father worshipped the devil and he sacrificed children."

"What did your mother have to do with it?"

"She was besotted with my father she had met him at fourteen. She had been brought up in Aberdeen and she had gone a little wayward. She met a man later to be my father who worked on the oil rigs. He was from Cyprus. He was a good-looking man and swept her off her feet. They ran away first to Sunderland undetected. When my mother was eighteen they married in Watford, where my dad had a job in a milk bottling factory."

"So where did it all go wrong?"

"Sadly my father had a keenness for girls between the ages of fourteen and sixteen. He killed his first victim, she was fifteen and a runaway. That is what he prayed on, because generally they wouldn't be missed. I will never forget her name or the pictures I was shown. Her name was Laura Golshin. She had run away from her family who lived in Surrey. Her father was a banker and her mother a social worker but she rebelled. She was so pretty. The social worker said my mother cooperated with the police with all the information. My father to this day says he is a superior being and has the given right to do what he did.

"So, what did he do?"

Poor Lee-Anne's eyes were red and swollen from the crying.

"He dismembered her body and they found her in Kiddling Wood just outside Watford. Her blood had been drained from her body. The police belief my father and mother drank this in some kind of ritual. They then placed the poor girl's arms and legs in a cross formation with her severed head in the middle. The torso they just threw away, that was later found half eaten by badgers and birds."

"Oh Lee-Anne, I am so sorry for you."

"There is a lot more to come, after each killing they moved on. The next poor girl was Eloise Bride, she befriended mum. Mum was working in a newsagents in Southampton and the girl had a Saturday job. At first they didn't know she was a run-away, but slowly it came out she was from Leicester, and had fallen out with her older brother so she just ran away. Dad saw his opportunity so they lured her to Gleadall Forest in Hampshire, on the pretence they were having a picnic. Once the picnic was laid out my father administered some kind of sleep drug which knocked her out. By now they had all the tools including full bunny suits, which they burnt after their horrendous acts of violence. Her body was found three weeks later with the same lay out; arms and legs cut off, head placed in the middle and the torso thrown away. Again her body had been drained of blood which my mother said she and my father drank.

There were three more incidents before they moved to Scotland. One in Cornwall, a girl called Alice Sergeant, another in Swindon a girl

called Micha Profac, a polish runaway
and finally before Scotland their last
victim. Susan Doon in Hull. They all
had the same thing done to them only
this time they were disturb by a
woman walking her two dogs. They
had almost finished drinking the
blood when one of the lady's dogs
came bounding over, and to the horror
of the dog walker who saw what my
parents had done. My mother said
they had no choice but to kill the
women, which my father did and he
also killed the dogs. My mother said
he strangled the woman and pulled the
dogs legs apart."

"Oh, you poor thing, carrying this
round with you all these years."

Lee-Anne carried on with her story.

"They decided it was time to move
North so they headed for Scotland.
They headed for a village called
Duloon. My mum by now was

pregnant with me. I am told the police believe the killings stopped well before she fell pregnant. After three years my father persuaded her to help him find a girl. They travelled to Edinburgh, apparently that's what my mother told the police. They left me in a hotel with sweets and pop and they paid the desk girl to keep popping into make sure I was ok. They told the girl that my father was meeting some old army pals and kids weren't allowed. They were from Gretna and they didn't have a baby-sitter.

They found a runaway which wasn't hard in Scotland. My mother said they took her for a meal and told her they were working for the Salvation Army and that they had lodges in Crangie Wood. My mother told the police that they told the girl she could get a shower, a bed for the night and a meal then they would take her back. You can imagine, the poor girl was ecstatic at this. My mother and father were very plausible. The girl's name was Patricia McCarran. This poor girl was the worst victim. My father drugged her and, for the only time, he raped a victim before killing her in the same way. Mother said she was sick in the bushes as the poor girl was beaten then raped repeatedly before he finally killed her. This time my mother couldn't drink the blood and my father hit her several times which he had never done before."

"Apparently from that day things went rapidly down-hill. My father made my mother drink blood from two more victims, Shelley Goldrick and Anna Stratch. Both girls were cut up and sacrificed with my parents drinking the blood.

"How were they caught?"

"After the last victim, my mother walked into the local police station with me and gave herself up. The local sergeant was amazed he had never seen or heard of anything like that in Duloon. I was taken into care."

"Were you never adopted?"

"Not until I was eleven. I spent seven years in the most horrendous homes being bullied by the staff and the kids. Eventually I was adopted by Mary and Len McDougall."

"So, were they ok with you?"

"Yes, they were lovely. Mary was a dinner lady and Len was a bus driver. They couldn't have children and I will always be grateful to them for giving me four happy years."

"So why didn't you invite them when we were getting married?"

"They were killed in a bus crash. Len was driving back from the Lake District and Mary had gone on holiday with him. A Polish lorry driver ran them off the road. Len was killed instantly and Mary died two days later."

"Oh Lee-Anne come here."

Daniel hugged her tightly.

"I know I have been awful since the abandoned wedding and losing the baby. I just went into this black hole and could not see myself climbing out. Today I realised, after being shitty with Millie, that you were going to finish things. I am so scared that I am like my father and mother, Daniel."

"Don't be silly, you are a loving caring person and I am not leaving you here. You are coming with me. Let's get away from here and go and stay with Aunty Millie. We could have gone to my house. It is only over the road but it's been rented out now, and besides I think Aunty Millie needs help."

"Daniel what if I am like my parents? You are better off without me."

"Listen lady, you are the best thing that ever happened to me, so I am not going to lose you. We will get through this I promise."

Daniel said he was going to have a shower and said he had one thing to do before he left Paisley. That was to find Murdo and his diaries. Daniel was showering while Lee-Anne started to cook dinner, when there was a loud knock on the door.

"I'm coming," Lee-Anne shouted. She opened the door but there was no sign of anyone. She was just about to shut the door, when she looked down and on the floor were Daniel's diaries that he had loaned to Murdo. She picked them up and looked to see if she could see anyone, but there was nobody there.

"Daniel, Daniel?"

"Hang on, just drying my hair."

Lee-Anne rushed into the bedroom to give Daniel his diaries.

"Wow I can't believe it. Did Murdo drop them off?"

"There was a knock at the door, but nobody was there but the diaries."

"I knew Murdo was a good type. He probably felt bad about bringing them back so didn't wait for us to answer the door. Right lady, I am going to phone the Green Tankard and tell them I quit and we are off down to London in the morning."

He hugged Lee-Anne and although Lee-Anne reciprocated the gesture, she still felt uneasy.

CHAPTER FIVE

Daniel phoned Billy who was very understanding and said if he ever came back there would be a job for him. Daniel was pleased with that. With all their worldly possessions in three suit cases they set off for the train-station and the trip to London. Daniel got two singles to St Pancras. They boarded the train with Lee-Anne insisting she had the window seat, which made Daniel smile, she seemed to be getting her mojo back he thought. As the train pulled away, standing in a doorway in a yellow suit and a blue bowler hat was Harkan. He smiled and doffed his hat. Lee-Anne saw him first.

"That's the dreadful man that touched my tummy when I was carrying our baby."

Daniel looked across with just enough time to see Harkan laughing and waving. Then the train was too far away. Daniel played it down and managed to get Lee-Anne back on track but he himself was worried. What was that all about he thought. On the journey to London Daniel and Lee-Anne laughed and joked. It was like their first date, the recent pressure seemed off them both. Daniel had decided he would surprise Millie so they got a taxi from St Pancras and arrived at Millie's house at 4.00pm. Daniel knocked on the door twice before he could hear Millie shuffling to the door. Millie screamed with emotion when she saw Daniel.

"Come in, oh and Lee-Anne too."

Lee-Anne could sense she wasn't over the moon to see her, but who could truthfully blame her Lee-Anne thought.

Once inside Millie started fussing as usual. She came out with a pot of tea and some cherry cake she had baked.

"I joined the local Women's Institute just for the company, so I always bake something to take. They are all such lovely people."

Lee-Anne thought it best to apologise for her moodiness last time she saw Millie. She explained that she had been depressed after the losing the baby then all the trouble at the wedding.

"Not a problem my dear, as long as you are feeling better. It's lovely to have you both here, it really is," Millie said. She seemed to have a second lease of life and skipped back to the kitchen to fill the tea pot. Lee-Anne got up to look out of the window across to Daniel's house and noticed some pictures.

"Who are they Daniel?"

"That's my Grandad and Uncle Jamie, Aunty Millie's husband."

Lee-Anne went to pick up the picture, but screamed as she picked it up, and immediately dropped the picture and the glass broke onto the hardwood floor.

"What happened Lee-Anne?"

"I don't know Daniel, the frame felt red hot."

"Let me look at your hands."

Daniel and Millie could not see anything on her hands that might suggest she had touched anything hot.

"Don't worry Lee-Anne, it's only a frame. I can get one tomorrow."

They settled down and watched a bit of TV with a bottle of wine. Daniel's mind was whirring, he still felt something was wrong. At least Lee-Anne seemed ok. That night Daniel and Lee-Anne had the front bedroom to sleep in. Millie was insistent that she make the bed up as she hadn't expected them down so quickly. It was almost one hour before

Daniel managed to get to sleep but when he did another dream started. Daniel found himself in the year 1958. He appeared to be a young man growing up in a normal family in Kentucky. His name was Stewey Lingfield. His father was a German immigrant and his mother was Italian. Her name was Ursula. Stewey was like any other all-American boy. He had just left school and was working at Millers Auto shop on 3rd and 5th Crimson Avenue. Stewey loved the cars and the new rock and roll craze that was sweeping America. He spent his time in Harold's Diner with his mates and the girls that followed them. Harold's Diner was owned by Harold Swanzy. For some reason everyone called him Billy. It was a nickname he had in the army and Billy, as everyone knew him, would always be telling anyone who would listen how he liberated France on his own!

Billy was a nice guy, the kids would take the mickey out of him, but they had a lot of respect for Billy. It was 6pm when Stewey arrived in his Cadillac. It was his pride and joy, red with a white flash, red leather seats and white wall tyres. His parents had bought it for him for his eighteenth birthday present. All the girls looked enviously at Stewey's Cadillac as he jumped out and headed into the Diner like something out of the American TV series Fonz.

"Large Americano Billy, two sugars and heavy on the cream."

"Coming up Stewey."

"Hey Stewey, how is it going?"

"Yeah good Charlie, what about you?"

"I want to talk to you about something."

"Go ahead."

"No, not here, privately."

Stewey and Charlie went to the back of the diner with the entire crowd doing wolf whistles.

"What's up Charlie?"

"I got a problem."

"Well I guessed that, what is it and how do I fit in?"

"I have only gone and got Peggy pregnant."

Stewey almost choked on his coffee.

"Who knows?"

"Only me you and Peggy. I have to tell her parents and will have to marry her Stewey."

"You sure will. So, what do you want from me?"

"Well you know I work in the liquor warehouse on Garfield Street."

"Yeah."

"Well a guy I know has offered me five hundred dollars if I knock off the warehouse."

"You serious?"

"Yeah and I wondered if you will help me. We could split the money, then I would put a deposit down on a house for me Peggy and the baby."

"No chance Charlie."

"Please Stewey. I can't do this on my own and you are my best mate."

"Hey man, I ain't doing a stretch for you."

"It won't happen. I have a spare set of keys for the warehouse and old Mikey sleeps all night. He doesn't walk round or anything."

"I don't know Charlie."

"Look what you could do with two hundred and fifty dollars, Stewey. You could get all that chroming done on the Cadillac."

"Stewey thought for a minute, "Ok but you sure there will be no hassle."

"Piece of cake buddy. I will let you know when and how. We best get back to the gang."

"You two lover boys been plotting a night in a Motel."

"Very funny Nina."

Daniel woke up. He could hear Millie shouting, "Breakfast Daniel."

Lee-Anne was already up. At least this dream didn't seem nasty. In fact he had quite enjoyed the experience Daniel thought.

"Did you sleep well Daniel?"

"Great thanks Aunty Millie, that bed is so comfy isn't it Lee-Anne?"

"Yeah so much better than the one in Paisley, Millie thank you."

"That's good then I have made you both eggs benedict, and if you want Daniel, I have spoken to Chris Moore. He is head of the banking floor where Uncle Jamie and your Grandad worked. He remembered your Grandad and said if you want to go and learn there is a job for you."

"Aunty Millie that is great, what do you think Lee-Anne?"

"It sounds perfect."

Daniel sensed Lee-Anne was probably missing Scotland as she wasn't over enthusiastic.

"Right I told Chris we would be there for ten. I took the liberty of getting your suit dry cleaned hope you don't mind?"

"That's my Aunty Millie, organised as usual. I won't let you down I promise."

"Hey Daniel, this is for you and Lee-Anne to start a new life. Me and Lee-Anne can go with you, then shall we go and do some girlie shopping while he works Lee-Anne?"

"That sounds good to me Millie."

Millie and Lee-Anne left a nervous Daniel at the trading floor and went off to enjoy their day. It was 6.30pm when Daniel arrived home. As Daniel walked in, Lee-Anne met him with a kiss which for the last three months had never happened.

"Hi Daniel," shouted Millie from the kitchen. "I am doing a steak and onion pie, is that ok?"

"Sounds great Aunty Millie. I'm starving and can't wait."

Millie laid the table while Daniel told Lee-Anne about his day learning to trade, he was genuinely excited.

"I feel like I am following in my grandad's shoes."

"That's great Daniel."

"Sorry, what sort of day have you had?"

Lee-Anne said Millie had taken her for lunch then she had shown her Buckingham Palace and the Houses of Parliament.

"Ok you two, dinner is served."

Millie put the pie down and that's when Daniel noticed she wasn't shaking.

"Aunty Millie, you aren't shaking."

"I know. I feel great. We were working round London and Lee-Anne and I linked arms and it was like a miracle, the shaking stopped."

"Wow you must be magic Lee-Anne," Daniel said.

Lee-Anne smiled then dropped the bombshell that she was going back to Scotland in the morning. Millie and Daniel looked shocked.

"Don't you think we should talk about this Lee-Anne?"

"No Daniel my mind is made up."

Lee-Anne was very matter of fact. Daniel had seen her like this before and knew she would not change her mind. Daniel looked at Millie and Millie knew not to say anything. With the evening meal somewhat awkward because of Lee-Anne's revelation they finished. Millie made an excuse she was seeing an old friend and she left them to discuss Lee-Anne's bombshell.

"Why are you going back to Paisley Lee-Anne?"

"Because I have to."

"So, are you saying we are finished?"

"I didn't say that. If you wish to stay with Millie that's your decision."

"This is all very matter of fact. I feel you are telling me we are done."

Lee–Anne looked at Daniel in a menacing way.

"You don't own me," she said.

"Oh, I give up, I'm going to see Patrick."

Daniel left calling his mate on the way. He wasn't sure if Lee-Anne would even be there when he got back.

Patrick and Daniel met at the Fallen Soldier on Fortune Street, a pub they frequented since they were sixteen because they got served.

"So how are you mate, and what the hell happened at your wedding? I was so pleased I was on holiday, with all those people dying mate."

"I know it was dreadful, and to be honest what with losing the baby as well, things have really gone downhill Pat."

"You are still with Lee-Anne though aren't you?"

"Don't know. She just announced she is going back to Paisley, so not sure if she will be there when I get back."

"Ok I'm sure she will be mate."

"You have more confidence than me. Anyway enough of that, do you still see Smudge and Arnie?"

"Smudge is working in Jersey and Arnie works for his dad in the haulage game."

"Blimey those two were legends, I always thought they were joined at the hip."

"Well you remember Alli Beresford?"

"The pretty lass from Whitechapel?"

"Yep the very one. Well Arnie started seeing her. Just after you left they got engaged and at the party he caught Smudge with her round the back."

"Oh crap, what happened?"

"All hell broke loose. Obviously the engagement was called off. Arnie and Smudge fell out, so I think that's why Smudge went to work away mate."

"Blimey it all happens down here doesn't it?"

"What you staring at Pat?"

"You ok mate? Both your eyes have gone blood red."

Daniel went to the bathroom and sure enough his eyes were blood red. This was all to do with Harkan. He knew it but how could he explain this to Patrick.

Daniel decided the best way would be to tell Patrick he didn't feel well and get back to Lee-Anne. He knew he had to go back to Grove and see if he could get back in time to find out more about his ancestor. Patrick said he would call him the next day to check he was ok.

Daniel called a taxi and arrived back at Millie's. He found Millie crying at the kitchen table and Lee-Anne gone. Millie was holding a note.

"Aunty Millie, what's the matter?"

She turned around and both her hands were shaking uncontrollably. Her face was also slightly skewed as if she had a stroke.

"When did this happen?"

"Only twenty minutes ago. I noticed the note from Lee-Anne, she has gone back to Paisley."

This is a mess Daniel thought.

"I am calling the doctor, Aunty Millie."

Daniel called for the doctor and he arrived two hours later.

Doctor Preston had been the family doctor for some thirty years so knew Millie very well. After an hour of thorough examination Dr Preston concluded that Millie was under major stress, and he advised she be taken to hospital.

"Your heart is racing Millie. You haven't had a stroke but your body seems to be trying to fight something, and I don't know what it is. Have you been to an African country?"

"I went with a friend to Tenerife but I had the shaking way before I went on holiday doctor."

"Your shaking isn't particularly a concern. I don't think that is life threatening but your body is fighting something Millie, and we have to find what it is. The ambulance is on its way."

"Can I ride in the ambulance with Aunty Millie, Doctor Preston?"

"Of course lad, not a problem, it may help to calm Millie."

Eventually the ambulance arrived to take Millie on the short journey to Lloyd George Hospital. Millie was rushed into theatre like a scene out of Casualty, she had drips and pipes everywhere. Daniel was pacing up and down.

After almost four hours a surgeon called him into his office with the sad news that Millie had passed away.

"Was it her heart?" Daniel asked.

"No, I'm afraid she choked."

"What do you mean?"

"Well some kind of green bile came out of her. We are analysing it in the lab. I have never seen anything like it. We did try several times to clear her air way and revive her but it was as if something was stopping us. I

am very sorry for your loss Mr Egan.
If you wish to sit a minute I can get
you a coffee."

"Could I see her please?"

"Of course, if you feel up to it?"

Daniel followed the surgeon down
to the side-ward where Millie had
been taken. She looked like a great
burden had been taken from her and
Daniel knew that all this was
connected to Grove. Daniel knew he
had to go back but first there was
Millie's funeral to organise.
Three days passed and Daniel
received a letter from Gerald Old,
Millie's solicitor. He had to go to
Camden the following day for the
reading of the will. Millie's funeral
was the following Monday. She had
asked to be buried. She didn't want
cremating she had said.

The following day Daniel arrived
at the solicitors. The office was
housed in an old corn warehouse. The

receptionist showed Daniel to Mr Old's office. Old was in his mid-sixties and was bald on top but had bushy white hair on the side, with long side burns a bit like Mr Pickwick, Daniel thought.

Old spoke.

"First of all, did you bring proof of your identity young man?"

Daniel produced his passport.

"Ok Mr Egan, this is the last will and testament of Millie Augustine Trench."

Daniel smiled Millie hated her middle name and he remembered how she said Uncle Jamie would tease her all the time about it. Augustine was her mother's name and her mother before her.

"Mrs Trench left all her estate which consists of her house, all her furniture and belongings to you. Also, her bank account with Barclays Bank totalling three hundred and twenty thousand pounds Mr Egan. She left her jewellery and her building society savings to a Miss Jennifer Makepeace. We as yet have been unable to find this person."

"That's because she is Mrs Jenny Logan now," and Daniel wrote down her address and telephone number for Old.

"We have to contact her Mr Egan, with regard to Mrs Trench's last will and testament, you cannot."

"I understand Mr Old, she is aware of my Aunty's funeral and she will be down for that."

"Ok well that concludes the reading of the will. All documents will be sent to you," and Old checked Daniel's address was still the same as Millie Trench's. Daniel confirmed.

"Could you also write down your bank account number etc so we may transfer funds Mr Egan."

GROVE

Daniel left the solicitors office feeling quite empty he now had nobody: his grandparents dead, his mother dead and now his Uncle Jamie and Aunty Millie. Daniel had tried to contact Lee-Anne but her phone seemed disconnected. He also tried the hotel but some stupid girl said she didn't know her, so Daniel asked to leave a message for Lee-Anne to call him.

Monday soon came and the day of the funeral. Jenny said she would be at the church. Millie had chosen to be buried at the church where she was christened and her parents were buried. Little Lambing was a small compact village in the Cotswolds. It had numerous thatched cottages, a small duck pond and a village pub where Daniel had arranged for the wake. He wasn't sure how many would be there but he catered for thirty.

The thirteenth century church had a beautiful stained-glass window depicting the feeding of the five thousand. Inside the church there were about eleven people when Daniel arrived. Jenny smiled across to him. This was possibly the lowest Daniel had been in his entire life. He felt anger towards Lee-Anne. He had heard nothing from her. How could she be so callous he thought? The vicar was a surprisingly young man. He stood up and started his sermon.

"Dearly beloved we are gathered here today in the Church of Saint Nicholas in our community of Little Lambing to celebrate the life of one of our own, Millie Augustine Trench, who sadly passed away and is now on her journey into the afterlife. I didn't know Millie personally although many of my parishioners knew Millie well when she was growing up. They tell me that Millie and her family were well respected in the community. Millie left Little Lambing to go to University and there she met her soul mate Jamie Trench. Together they had many happy years until Jamie was tragically killed in a road accident. I would like you to all stand for our first hymn 'For Those In Peril On The Sea'.

The vicar did his best to sing, as the congregation was so small it was never going to be rapturous. With the hymn finished the vicar introduced Daniel to do his eulogy. Daniel straightened his tie and made his way to the pulpit, clearing his throat he began.

"My Aunty Millie was like my mum for so many years until my real

mum came out of a coma. Aunty
Millie brought me up she gave me
values and a work ethic. Aunty Millie
never had a bad word for anyone. She
always said I was to treat people how
I wished to be treated. I remember
coming home from school one day
upset because a boy two years older
than me had been bullying me. She
made me point him out to her when he
was in a McDonalds with his friends.
I will never forget how she made the
boy see the error of his ways and by
the time she had finished, his friends
were laughing at him for bullying a
much younger boy. That boy from
that day looked after me at school and
we became firm friends all thanks to
Aunty Millie. Aunty Millie was kind
generous and enjoyed life but when
Uncle Jamie passed away she lost a
big part of her life.

GROVE

Well today beautiful Aunty Millie, you will be reunited with Uncle Jamie and happiness will be yours now."

Daniel paused for a minute, a small tear trickling down his cheek.

"Forever when I see a kind act I will think of this lady for she epitomised honesty and caring that I will take with me on my life journey."

Daniel folded the paper he had written his speech on and stepped down from the pulpit. Jenny was crying as she looked over to poor Daniel. The final hymn 'Onward Christian Soldiers' was sung and Daniel and Jenny followed the coffin to the grave side. They both comforted each other as the coffin was lowered into the ground. Jenny had bought a red rose for her and Daniel to drop on the coffin.

Back at the village pub, The Black Sheep, everyone from the congregation came and with the vicar, that made twelve people. Jenny and Daniel sat talking.

"What are you going to do Daniel?"

"I think I will go back to Paisley."

"I didn't see your girlfriend, Lee-Anne isn't it? Millie was telling me what a pretty girl she is."

"We split up Jenny, not sure how it will all work out to be honest."

"Well you will know when you have the right one. I did."

Jenny was very tempted to tell Daniel who his father was, with him now not having any family. Out of the blue Daniel asked the question, "Do you know who my father is, Jenny."

"Yes, I do Daniel."

"Will you tell me?"

"If you wish me to."

"Who is he then? Was he just a one night stand?"

"No, it was never meant to be that Daniel. It was just the way things worked out. He never knew of your existence."

"So, he doesn't know he has me?"

"Not to my knowledge. So, what is his name and where does he live?"

"The last time I saw him he ran an estate and a hotel in Derbyshire. His name is Matt Babington."

Daniel almost fell of his chair.

"Did you say Babington?"

"Yes why?"

"Just remember reading a story in school about Mary Queen of Scots."

"You have lost me Daniel."

Daniel didn't say anymore but he knew this was somehow all entwined, but how and why he had no idea.

CHAPTER SIX

Daniel thanked everyone and went back to Millie's place. It seemed empty without that cheery smile and the smell of her wonderful cooking. Although he wasn't drunk he had certainly given Millie a send-off. He kicked off his shoes and lay on the bed he was soon fast asleep and back in his dream.

Charlie had arranged to pick up Stewey at midnight and drive him to Garfield Street and the liquor warehouse. Charlie reversed the brown truck into the yard. It was deathly silent with no sign of life. Charlie threw the keys to Stewey and he undid the lock. Once inside they could hear Mikey snoring. So slowly they carried box after box of whisky to the truck until it was full. Stewey had got inside the passenger seat of the truck while Charlie was locking up. Suddenly there was a loud bang and Charlie came running. He jumped in the truck and drove like a maniac.

"What the hell happened? Did I hear a gun shot?"

"He saw me Stewey, Mikey saw me."

"What?"

"I was locking the door and he came and he called my name. I had no choice.

"What did you do?"

"I shot him, dead men don't talk Stewey. I had no choice."

"I didn't sign up for this Charlie."

"Too late hot shot, we are real gangsters now."

Stewey was in shock as they drove into the wooded rest area. A truck was waiting.

"Ok boys," the head of the gang said, "let's see what Pixie and Dixie have managed to do?"

"Can I have a word Mr?"

"Exactly punk, Mr that's what you call me clear?"

"Yes Sir."

"Now what's your problem?"

Charlie told him what he had done at the warehouse. The man laughed, "So what do you want me to do?"

"Can you clean it up and get rid of the body so it looks like he wasn't at work?"

"Sure, I can do that wise guy, but it will cost you five hundred bucks."

"But that's all me and my partner are getting for tonight."

"Well I guess that's tough. Now take it or leave it."

Charlie looked at Stewey, "We have no choice man."

Stewey shrugged his shoulders. Over the coming months Daniel's dream about Stewey carried on. Charlie and Stewey were now so far in, there was no way out. It was early

GROVE

August when Stewey and Charlie were summoned to meet the Godfather, Jimmy the Drink, although nobody he called him that for fear of retribution. He had got his name by drowning people he didn't like, or anybody who crossed him, and boy was he ruthless. The two boys were flown to Dallas Texas. By now both boys had left home and had plenty of money as they were climbing the criminal tree. They were taken to a palatial house on the outskirts of Dallas, it was more of a ranch. They were shown into a room with a large glass chandelier and big leather settees. A portly man, clearly Jimmy the Drink, sat behind an oak desk puffing a big Cuban cigar.

"Sit down gentlemen."

Stewey and Charlie sat down directly behind them stood two henchmen.

"Right I will get straight on it. I want you to do something for me."

"Anything Sir," said Charlie.

"I want you to shoot the President, JF Kennedy, when he visits Dallas."

Charlie stood up. "No way, I ain't shooting anybody."

Jimmy the drink nodded and two shots rang out. They just shot Charlie in the back of the head.

"Right young man," Jimmy said to Stewey, "can you help me?"

Stewey knew his choices were limited.

"Ok, right from now until the day you will practise eight hours day. We will supply the gun and shells."

Jimmy then stood up shook Stewey's hand and showed him out.

Every day until that fateful day Stewey was taken to the back of the house and he practised. He got so good that he could shoot a button in

the dead centre. Stewey was given his
final instructions by Jimmy. He never
asked why? He just knew he had no
choice. They did tell him that he
would be the shooter and that they
had created a Patsy who would shoot
from the library, but who couldn't hit
a barn door from three yards

It was November 22nd 1963. Stewey
had been taken to Dallas. His
instruction was to shoot Kennedy in
the head. He was told to shoot twice
and the Patsy would shoot once from
the library to create the panic. Stewey
was told to fire from behind a fence
are above a grassy knoll. Stewey was
told that two police officers would be
aware of him and they would get him
away.

It was 12.15pm when Stewey got in
position behind the fence near the
road. Stewey could see people waving

flags and posters supporting the President. Stewey could not believe what he was about to do. Even after all those practise sessions he was still very nervous. This man is the President of the United States he thought. It was 12.28pm when he saw the President's cavalcade turn the corner. As the President's vehicle slowly worked its way down Dealey Plaza towards Stewey. The first shot was fired. Although Stewey heard it Jimmy the Drink was right the Patsy could not hit a barn door. Stewey let his first shot go which hit Texas Governor John Connelly. Panic was setting in. People were screaming. Stewey had one clear shot and he took it, the President slumped forward.

Stewey wasn't hanging about. The two policemen bundled him in a car with its sirens in full flow. It didn't matter they were going the other way.

The police men took Stewey to the train station and told him they had a train ticket for New York for him and they would take care of the rifle.

Stewey arrived at Penn Street station still in shock at what he had done. He found a room in Times Square and the following day the papers were full of the President and the arrest of Lee Harvey Oswald. His arrest was initially for killing police officer J D Tippit some forty five minutes after the President's shooting. His arrest was soon escalated to the shooting and subsequent murder of the President.

Stewey didn't know what to do when Oswald said he was a patsy. In a small bar just off Times Square he knew how his life was in real danger. He saw Jack Ruby shoot Oswald. He knew Jack Ruby who was a frequent visitor to the Dallas ranch of Jimmy the Drink, and he had often spoken to Stewey.

Daniel woke from his dream he was sweating and confused. Daniel never had the same dream again and with weeks going by, he decided to go and introduce himself to his genetic father, Matt Babington. After searching on the internet he found him. He lived in Leaf, a village in Derbyshire. Daniel took a picture of his mum that Millie had on her fireplace. It was a two and a half hour drive from London to the little village of Leaf. Daniel had booked a room at the Jiggly Glass pub and he arrived at 6.15pm.

On arrival Daniel was met by the landlady.

"Good evening Sir. I see you have booked with us for three nights. I am sure you will love Leaf and the surrounding villages. My name is Sandra Hodgekiss. Breakfast is 6.30am-9.30am."

Sandra showed Daniel to his room which was delightful.

"If you require lunch or dinner we do both in the bar."

Sandra left giving Daniel his key, which had a bright red rubber ball attached so you didn't lose the key.

After settling into the comfortable accommodation. Daniel was pleasantly surprised, he had only paid eighty pounds a night and this accommodation in London would have been nearer two hundred pounds. Daniel changed and headed down to the bar. There was a mix of locals and what he thought were out of town diners.

"What would you like Sir?" said the pretty girl working the bar.

"Oh um, I'm not sure."

Just then the old guy sitting at the bar gave his opinion.

"Tha wants Pedigree lad, none better."

"Thank you, I'll have a pint of that then and take one for my beer critic."

"That's good on yer lad."

Daniel offered his hand to his new-found friend.

"Daniel Egan."

"Eric Young," said the man.

"What brings thee ta Peak District lad? Are tha walking?"

"Well no, actually it's a long story."

Daniel thought using the family tree thing might be a good idea.

"Tracing my family tree Eric."

"My nephew did that. We only had a bloody Highway man in ours. He was hung at Derby. Guess he wasn't any good at it," and Eric laughed. "So, who do you think you are related to then Daniel?"

"Not sure to be honest, just know we have some history. Leaf House came up in my searches."

"What the Babington place?"

Daniel played dumb.

"Babington? Sorry I don't understand. One of my ancestors had been a groom there I believe."

"Well at least you aren't related to Babington. What an arse. I worked for his father for thirty years as a game-keeper and then Matt Babington takes over turns that beautiful house into a hotel and spa, and I was no longer needed. Speak of the devil, he's just walked in."

Matt Babington was with a woman and two other adults. One Daniel thought was perhaps in her twenties, and a boy who looked about sixteen. Daniel knew straight away that Babington was his father the resemblance was uncanny.

Daniel decided to leave confronting Babington until he was better prepared. He questioned Eric further.

"Who's doing all that loud cackling in the restaurant?"

"That will be Babington letting everyone know the Lord of the Manor is in the building, bloody tosser."

Eric clearly wasn't a fan of Daniel's biological father. A few more beers followed before Daniel called it a night. The weather wasn't the best during the night, with heavy rain lashing against the old wooden windows of his room.

The following morning Daniel went down for his breakfast and was sharing a table with a gentleman and his wife from Demdyke in Lincolnshire. They talked to Daniel about their reason for being there. They said they came every year on the anniversary of their son's death. He had been a keen motorcyclist and had come to the Peak district over many years. It was a fateful day in May 1991when he met with his demise on a famous twisting road leading from Cranford to Gilligan Mill. They told him the twisting roads were, and are, still used by the bikers to test their skills. Their son had done this many times but on this particular Sunday Morning he didn't realise the local quarry was working. He met a lorry on the wrong side of the road and was killed instantly. Daniel felt sorry for the couple for all those years they had come up to the Peak district to place flowers at the scene of the crash.

Penny and Michael Swift, as they had introduced themselves, were in their late fifties. They had asked Daniel why was he in Derbyshire, so he trotted out the family tree story. Penny told him he should visit Ribery

Castle a local landmark while he was here. Daniel finished his breakfast and thanked Penny and Michael for the information and wished them a safe journey back to Lincolnshire, as they had said they were leaving after breakfast.

Arriving back at his room Daniel opened his laptop and researched Babington and then Ribery Castle. It was with surprise that his research turned up that Matt Babington also owned Ribery Castle. With this in mind he decided to head for the castle first. The castle was perched at the top of a peak overlooking Leaf and the small hamlet of Ribery from where it took its name. Daniel left his car in the hamlet and walked the small hill up to the castle. After the storms during the night the castle was now bathed in sunshine. It stood majestically looking down on Daniel as he walked up to it.

The castle had a farm shop, a coffee shop and a small visitor centre. These were all housed in what was originally the kitchen gallery. Much of the castle's interior had disappeared overtime. It had a chequered history. It was built in 1862 by a local entrepreneur Sir James Markham, for his French wife, Adelais Gustov. Sir James Markham only lived there for one year. His wife had a further three years living in the castle before she succumbed to fever. The castle was then sold to the government in 1911. It became a hospital for soldiers that had been injured at the front. From 1934 until the Second World War it had fallen into disrepair, but was used again as a treatment hospital for the soldiers. While Daniel was reading about the castle a strange professor looking man spoke.

"Shame the Babingtons have it now. That's the end for the castle as we know it young man."

Daniel was a little shocked at the man's comment so questioned it.

"Why? Who are the Babingtons?" he asked.

"Now Sir, that is a long story. Have you time for a tea?"

"Yes, I would like that. I am Daniel Egan and you are Sir?"

"My name is Christian Berwick. I live in Ribery. Would you like to have a coffee at my house Daniel?"

Daniel thought it all a bit strange but he was keen to find out about Matt Babington so he accepted this strange man's invitation.

Daniel and Christian walked from the castle down a small lane to Mr Berwick's house. The house was very pretty with wisteria clinging to the south facing façade. The little wooden gate opened into the front garden. It was like something from Homes and Gardens that his Aunty Millie loved reading. A small lady of perhaps only five feet two in stature met them at the half glass paned front door.

"This is my wife, Daniel."

"Pleased to meet you Mrs Berwick."

"Please call me Sarah. Come now let me make you afternoon tea."

"Well that is very kind of you Sarah."

Christian showed Daniel into the pretty sitting room. All the walls had pictures of Ribery castle. Sarah brought through the afternoon tea. Christian became quite serious and stated his immense dislike for the Babington family and in particular Matt. Daniel could not help feeling a fraud in the man's house.

Christian stated that the castle came up for sale some three years ago and nobody wanted Babington to have it because of the upheaval they all knew it would cause. Daniel questioned their concerns. Christian explained that Babington bought it and immediately applied to knock down the castle ruins and build an executive house on the land.

"He wasn't successful then Christian?"

"Not to knock it down, but I honestly don't think that was the real plan. Hence the bit of showboating at the castle, he wants the planners to think he cares for its heritage. Last week he put in plans for sixty four flats and he got it passed. Ok there are restrictions, but the man will make a fortune and the castle and this beautiful hamlet will be lost in the mayhem that will follow. So, you can see why everyone dislikes the man I hope you don't find him in your family tree Daniel. He is a ruthless man and only thinks of himself." Christian and his wife showed him old pictures of Ribery and he could see what they were saying. They then showed him carnival pictures in the early fifties and there was a picture of the man that was his Grandad, Edward Babington.

Sarah laughed, "You actually look like them Daniel, sorry for that."

Daniel laughed and brushed it off. It was almost 8.00pm when he left Ribery. Christian and Sarah waved him off and said he could visit anytime he was in the Peak District. As Daniel drove back to Leaf through the country lanes he looked back on his day. Could his biological father be so bad?

Back at the pub Daniel showered and went down into the bar. He wasn't hungry after the enormous afternoon tea.

"Had a good day Mr Egan?" said the landlady.

"Yes, I have been to Ribery Castle and met some really nice people."

She leaned forward, "I am guessing you got the Babington story. He isn't well liked round here Mr Egan. I am polite with him because of the trade but he is obnoxious. He really thinks he is the lord of the manor."

Daniel just smiled and ordered his pint of Pedigree. It was quite quiet in the bar so at 10.30pm he retreated to his room.

Daniel wished he had not bothered to come to Derbyshire to speak with Matt Babington, so he decided to check out the next day and head back to Paisley and what that had to offer. He didn't need a father figure in his life, he hadn't had one so far, so what the hell he thought.

The following morning after breakfast Daniel checked out and started his journey up to Paisley. The weather had changed yet again and the journey which should have taken five hours took almost eight. Daniel arrived and went straight to the Green Tankard to see Billy. Billy was over the moon and immediately offered Daniel is old job back and accommodation after Daniel explained about Lee-Anne.

CHAPTER SEVEN

Two months passed there had been no dreams and no contact with Lee-Anne. Daniel knew it was time to visit Grove again. The following Saturday was his day off so he planned to go then. He wasn't sure what might happen but he was sure something was telling him to go there.

Early Saturday morning Daniel headed out of Paisley for Grove. The place was eerie but somehow Daniel felt he belonged. He parked his car at the top of the village and headed down the dusty road towards the church. St Matthews Church seemed to be the only place in Grove that appeared normal. He walked down the church path as he had done many times now. Daniel's heart was thumping so hard it was almost jumping out of his chest. He turned the key in the old lock and cautiously entered the church. As he had hoped, the old lady was sitting praying in the oak pews halfway down the aisle. Daniel never questioned how she got in the church when it was locked, but he was pleased to see her all the same. Daniel sat next to her and at first she didn't look up, she just kept praying. When she had finished she turned to Daniel. Her eyes were green and they looked tired.

"Why have you come back?"

Daniel wasn't expecting this question. He gulped and gestured that he felt the need.

"You are not being a wise man Daniel," she said.

"Why is that? Please explain."

The old lady turned to Daniel and held his hand tightly.

"I told you, only you can save humanity and you had the chance."

"What, kill my ancestor? What would that have done? He is already dead."

She smiled, "you are naïve Daniel."

"Look since my mother died my whole life has been crap. I have to find out what the hell is going on. Will you take me back to Grove?"

"If you come back, I can't guarantee you will ever get back to this time Daniel. I don't think you should take that chance. Live your life, you chose not to change the world last time. Just go and live your life."

Daniel felt her hand leave his hand and she was gone. Daniel sat in the church for maybe an hour just trying to get his head round all of this.

As he got up to leave he could hear somebody whispering his name.

"Daniel Egan, Daniel Egan." There standing in the pulpit was Harkan.

"What the hell do you want?"

"Nice greeting for a friend Mr Egan."

"Let's get one thing straight I am not your friend."

Harkan laughed but in a weird way. He was dressed in a red overcoat with yellow trousers and blue plimsolls.

"Let me tell you something Mr Egan."

"I don't need you to tell me anything," Daniel said and he got up to walk away.

After leaving the pew he felt a force stopping him moving forward.

"Problem Mr Egan?"

"Who are you?"

"Look on me as your trainer."

"What?"

"Trainer in the finer things of life and I really don't want to fail Mr

Egan, because that isn't an option for my boss."

"So, who is your boss?"

"All will be revealed once I am confident of your support Mr Egan."

"Stop talking in riddles. Why did you come to our apartment? Lee-Anne was pregnant and you touched her stomach and she miscarried."

"Look, all things will be revealed eventually."

Harkan just disappeared in front of Daniel. Daniel had never felt so low. He knew something big was coming but he didn't know when or why.

Daniel locked the church and walked the short walk back to his car. Now what was he to do? Daniel got back to the Green Tankard and ordered a double whisky. From behind him a voice said, "Best get me a Dewey then laddie." Daniel turned around, sure enough it was Murdo.

"Where the hell have you been and how come nobody knew you when I asked?"

"Get your whisky laddie and let's have a seat."

"So Daniel, you thought meeting me that first night was a coincidence. How wrong were you.?"

"What do you mean?"

"Let's say I am protecting you from some very naughty people."

"Murdo, help me out here."

"Ok Daniel, sit comfortably and I will begin. My name is Murdoch Murray I was born in 1490 in Grove. My parents were Alan and Bridie Murray. I was a twin and that's where my story begins. My brother James was killed by an Egan child when he was eight. From that day my life changed. They said he had drowned while fishing but I knew they had drowned him."

"Just a minute Murdo, are you saying you are a time traveller or something?"

"Well not so much a time traveller but a time creator."

"Now you have totally lost me Murdo."

"Well let me explain. Let's say you fancied being a pirate, then I give you this stone."

Murdo showed Daniel a well-worn pebble. You hold this and concentrate and you will be transported to where you want to go. The only problem is if you lose the stone there is no way back!"

"It's a fantastic story but pray tell me how this fits in with my problems?"

"Well you see that is one of the reasons I befriended you. When you told me your story and of course your families story I realised I had to read the diaries. I do know you are on a crash course to hell, and I am not sure the force taking you there even I can stop."

Daniel sat with a bemused look on his face.

"Let me go back to 1498. Your ancestor Dermot Egan had come to our prosperous village in 1497. At first everything was fine. Slowly Egan began to take control during the bad winter. Emotions ran high, men couldn't work which meant families were starving. If you add to that they had no fuel, it was a trying time. Dermot Egan would brag about his plentiful table and you never saw their chimney without smoke coming from it. He would walk down the street like Johnny Big Time. People would beg him for food. It didn't matter if it was man, woman or child he would lash out with his boot. People were weak, cold and desperate and slowly the village population dwindled. When my brother was murdered by Seamus Egan I was ripped apart. My brother and I were very close. I was at home helping my mother with chores. I was no good at fishing but brother James had a canny knack of knowing where to drop his line. Without James up to that point, we would have starved like the rest of the village."

"I can recall quite vividly my father sitting in the armchair and me and Ma sweeping round him, when I suddenly stopped and had this vision. I could see everything. My brother had four fish, not big ones, but enough to keep us from starving for a couple of days. Seamus Egan who would have been about twelve at the time, sneaked up behind my brother and pushed his head underwater. James was no match for the older boy and was soon dead. Seamus just threw his limp body in the snow and took the fish. I can see him now laughing as he walked through the village with the fish."

"So how did the time travel, sorry time creator, come about?"

"That's for another day Daniel."

"Can we meet tomorrow please Murdo? You are my only hope."

"I'm not sure I am that Daniel, but ok, say 3.00pm here at the Green Tankard."

Daniel watched Murdo leave and decided to follow this unlikely time creator as he called himself. From a short distance he watched Murdo make his way through the town. Strangely nobody seemed to know him, yet he said when they first met that he had lived here all his life. Something wasn't adding up he thought. Murdo took a left which led him to the cobbled path leading to Brook Street. Daniel watched Murdo move toward the book shop. At this point Daniel sprinted down the cobbles, but as he arrived by the six steps that were used as the staging for the hangings, there was no sign of Murdo. What Daniel had known as a book shop opposite was also as before with no actual shop to enter. People can't just disappear, there must be a logical reason behind all this.

As Daniel started walking back a couple in the late sixties were walking towards him.

"Have you seen any ghosts they asked?"

Daniel wanted to say yes but he just politely smiled and hurried on his way back to the Green Tankard. On the way Daniel called for fish and chips and ate them walking in the rain on the way back. Once in his room he quickly showered, then filled in his diary with what Murdo had told him. Then he tried to relate what it all meant. Nothing made any sense other than Murdo knew his ancestor. Daniel began to wonder if Murdo, after reading the diaries, was playing a game.

The following morning Billy asked if Daniel could help to bottle up and would he mind doing the 5.00pm to 11.00pm shift. This was perfect he thought, he could go and see Lee-Anne and try and sort things out. Then he could have a couple of hours with Murdo before his shift started. With the bottling up done he headed for the apartment.

Daniel rang the door-bell until his finger was sore. Finally he tried his key but it didn't fit. With no choice, he headed for the William Wallace hotel thinking Lee-Anne may have got her job back. One of Lee-Anne's friends was on reception.

"Hello Sally."

Sally seemed taken aback.

"Is Lee-Anne back working here?"

"No Daniel we haven't heard from her since she went to London with you."

"We split and she told me she was coming home."

"What happened to you two, you were so in love?"

"The wedding and losing the baby put so much pressure on us Sally."

"I am so sorry, you were a lovely couple. If she gets in touch I will let you know."

"Thanks Sally. I am back at the Green Tankard."

"Ok, well me and Phil will pop in and see you soon. Take care now," she said.

Daniel headed back it was now almost 3.00pm. True to form Murdo was sitting at the bar with a glass of his favourite tipple Dewey.

"Hiya laddie, don't mind if I do. Make it a large one. Let's sit over there."

Daniel was really beginning to think that Murdo was somehow connected or just playing a game. The usual presumptive Murdo he thought. Daniel carried his pint of heavy and the double Dewey over to the table Murdo had chosen.

"Ok part two," Murdo said. "You asked me about the time creator. At my brother's funeral, which was nothing to be honest, we couldn't have a wake, we had no food. But we did have a service at St Matthews's church. The congregation looked dreadful. Being a little boy I was inquisitive so nipped outside to look at the gravestones. Although I was only eight I could read really well. By a grave stone for a Jean Crick stood a woman all in black. Well when I say stood, she was stooped, she was dressed all in black. When she turned around her face had more lines than Scotland's railway system. For some reason I wasn't scared, to this day I don't know why but I wasn't. She looked at me and spoke so softly like an angel.

"So finally you come to see me Murdoch. I am sorry for your family's loss. I too have known this terrible emptiness. I have something for you and she produced the stone."

Daniel thought it more like a pebble, but hey who was going to split hairs on this fantastic story?"

"She put it in my hand then said these words 'You jach juntúul paal yéetel juntúul nuxi' responsabilidad. Le k'aas le ti' tuláakal tu'ux ka mixba'al asab u Saatalen. Ma' meyaj le tuunicha' tak u decimocuarto k'aaba'. Sostenga u le tuunicho' yéetel jach yaan tu'ux k'áat. Chéen u páajtal

232

utilizar le tuunicho' Kanp'éel Óoxten
túun k'a'abéet a kaxtik le máak
úuchuk utia'al encendido xan. "Le
máak ti' u pasa a liberará yéetel kun
yúuchul kuuch ti' u person elegido'"

"She then translated what she said
into English 'You are a little boy now
with a big responsibility. Evil is
everywhere and none more than
Grove. Don't use this stone until your
fourteenth birthday. Hold the stone
and it will take you wherever you
wish. You can only use the stone four
times then you must find the right
person to pass it on too. The person
you pass it onto will release you and
the burden will pass to your chosen
person'"

"You can now see why I had to
read your diaries. When I saw the
same language being used I knew you
were the one."

"What is this burden Murdo?"

"'The Evil', they search out good people that may have done something wrong and then they test them."

"In what way?"

"Mainly with dreams. You see Daniel, your ancestor Dermot Egan was evil, but looking at your diaries the family must have gone back to Ireland. By the time your family travelled back to England and your father was born in Liverpool the family was free of 'The Evil', and your grandfathers parents possibly didn't even know about 'The Evil'.

"This is so confusing Murdo."

"Aye I know that laddie. I have lived with this crap for over six hundred years waiting for you, the chosen one to rid the world of 'The Evil'."

"But how do I do this Murdo?"

"I was told you would be tested. I am sure you thought you were dreaming like your mother and

grandfather, but you weren't, you were actually there. Tell me about your dreams and your actions but first laddie a large Dewey might help things."
Daniel smiled and ordered another pint of heavy for himself and a large Dewey for Murdo as requested. The bar had filled up as Daniel sat down with Murdo.

"So, tell me Daniel, how have you been tested?"

Daniel took a good swig from his beer and began his story thus far.

"My first dream was about a boy called William Dowd, he was a servant of Anthony Babington I didn't know at the time but he was my ancestor."

"What evil were you summoned to commit?"

"Babington had me take a letter. It was in regard of Mary Queen of Scots and a plot to put her on the throne of England."

"Let me guess Daniel, you failed?"

"Yes, but how do you know?"

"All these things are a test to see if you are actually 'The Evil'."

"What do you mean Murdo?"

"In Liam Egan's diaries does he kill?"

"Well yes, he has no choice."

"Wrong answer, we all have a choice. In your mother's diaries did she kill?"

"Well yes again, she had no choice. You have read the diaries Murdo!"

"Let me tell you something Daniel, before 'The Evil' can be defeated you will learn about choice. Now laddie second dream?"

"I was Thomas Bent a butcher's apprentice in the plague village of Eyam. I was eventually murdered by my master Mr Snoddy.

"You don't have to tell me why Daniel. I pretty much know. You see 'The Evil' could see you weakening at that point."

Daniel felt concerned at how the dreams were being interpreted by Murdo.

"So, onto dream three. Quite a big one I believe?"

Who really was Murdo Daniel thought?

"Adolf Hitler, tell me this dream Daniel."

"I was a soldier in the first world war. My name was Harry Skills and I could have killed Adolf Hitler."

"But you chose not to and this was your defining moment for 'The Evil'. Because you unleashed so much harm and terror on the world with this act, that 'The Evil' now saw you in the same light as Dermot Egan your ancestor. dream four Daniel please."

GROVE

"This is the weird one Murdo. I came out of the church and was taken by Mr Skillet a resident of Grove when my ancestor Dermot Egan lived there. He took me to tree in the churchyard and told me to sit in it and suddenly it was like I had been put in a washing machine. Everything began spinning and I found myself in Grove. I was there quite a long time and Skillet insisted I kill my ancestor. I couldn't bring myself to do it Murdo."

"That was your biggest mistake because 'The Evil' then saw your weakness, and knew then that 'The Evil' could have you."

"What do you mean?"

"Going through your dreams Daniel, you have had the chance to change history and crush 'The Evil', but each time you have been weak and let 'The Evil' take over. Ultimately you will pay the price."

At this point Daniel became upset and his voice quavered in desperation.

"What do I do Murdo?"

"I canna tell thee laddie, all I know is I am no longer on 'The Evil's radar. You are now very much in their sights. I canna help thee. I have given you the stone but unless you are lucky and there is somebody after you to pass it on too then I am afraid Daniel you are doomed. You see Daniel you have been there on four separate occasions, and your actions have not justified good but have justified 'The Evil'."

Murdo said he needed the toilet and left Daniel pondering on what looked like a bleak future. Ten minutes had passed with no sign of Murdo. Daniel was worried so he went to the toilet to see if he was ok. The toilets were empty, Murdo had gone. He asked everyone who he thought knew Murdo if they had seen

him but it was if he never existed.
Everybody he asked denied knowing
him.

Daniel carried the shiny pebble with
him at all times, but had never used it.
Fear of the unknown and what Murdo
had told him was enough to put
Daniel off.

CHAPTER EIGHT

Daniel tried to get on with his life. Lee-Ann had seemed to disappear out of his life, there was no sign of her. Months past and it was Christmas Eve. Daniel volunteered to work because he had no real friends, only the locals that came in most nights. He had tried to put everything out of his mind and it appeared to work. Although he wondered why Murdo hadn't asked about the fifth dream. He hadn't had anymore dreams and life was ok.

Billy had put on an eighties disco and the Green Tankard was packed. It was while he was collecting glasses that he noticed a tall girl staring at him. Daniel smiled, in his mind she looked like the actress Kiera Knightley.

"Hi, I'm Daniel," he said at the tall girl.

"Oh, I'm Anouska," she said. Daniel put down the glasses and pulled up a chair.

"What a pretty name, you are clearly not Scottish?"

"No, I'm part Danish and part Welsh. My father was from Denmark and my mother was from Wales. You are not Scottish either are you?" she said.

"No, I'm from London originally. Look I get off at twelve do you fancy meeting for a drink somewhere?"

"Where Daniel?"

"There is a small bar on Pilchard Street, it's called The Old Musket. I can be there for 12.10am if you want?"

"Ok I will see you there."

Daniel left Anouska feeling quite pleased with himself. He hadn't bothered with girls since Lee-Ann but perhaps it was time to move on. He was thinking that was something Aunty Millie would have said as he skipped back behind the bar. Anouska and her mates left soon afterwards but not before Anouska had whispered she would see Daniel at 12.10am.

Daniel finished his shift and explained to Billy about his date and he let him get off. Rain had turned to snow and the town centre was full of Christmas revellers singing Christmas Carols. Most of them struggling to even say the correct words but it was all harmless merriment.

Daniel arrived at The Old Musket and could see Anouska sat at the window. She waved shyly and Daniel waved. Once inside Anouska stood up and Daniel took his chance pecking her on the cheek as he greeted her. He got them both a drink and they sat talking. For almost two hours they laughed as they watched the drunken revellers having snowball fights and falling over in the white carpet of snow.

"Where do you live Anouska and what a pretty name?"

"I have an apartment near the William Wallace Hotel. My name was the same as my Russian ancestor, her name was Anouska Deblinker."

Anouska started telling Daniel her story how her Great-great-grandfather and Great–great-grandmother had fled the Russian revolution. She said her Great-great-grandfather had been a close confidante at the court of the Czar Nicolas the second, and he had told her Great-great-grandfather to take his family and leave Russia just before it all started.

"Wow Anouska how interesting."

"There is more Daniel. Initially they lived in Italy where in a small village called Sammia. Their daughter my Great-Grandmother met and married Gino just before the war started in Italy and they fled to England. My Great-grandfather father hated the Fascists so he took us to England. My Great-grandfather then joined the RAF but was killed on a bombing raid over Germany in 1944. They had only one child, a girl aged eighteen months she was my Grandmother. My Grandmother's name was Sophia Del Pillo. She grew up in orphanages because in 1951 at the age of nine her mother died of heart failure. So she ended up in numerous orphanages until she was eighteen in 1962. She didn't have a particularly great life. At eighteen she was tossed out into the big wide world. She saw and advert for a hotel job in Paisley so she took her chance and went to Scotland to start her new life. She met and married Alex Cameron a doctor in 1973. They had

one child, a girl. Her name was Elli
Maria Cameron. Elli was my Mum
and she had a charmed life. They had
money and prominence in society
here in Scotland with her father being
a doctor.

Mum was a bit of a rebel but
eventually settled down. In 1994 she
married my father Alan Duxbury.
They had me a year later in 1995. My
mum decided she wanted to call me
after my ancestor. So here I am,
Anouska Deblinker Duxbury, and I
am training to be a surgeon.

"Now you know my story, what
about you Daniel?"

Daniel thought this could be fun.
Did he tell the real story or the basic
story? He went for the basic,
frightened the truth could well drive
her away.

GROVE

"Ok my name is Daniel Egan I am from London. My story is nothing like yours Anouska."

Anouska smiled, her long dark hair complementing her beautiful pearly smile.

"From what I can gather we are from Ireland originally. Then the family ended up in Liverpool before my grandfather Liam Egan moved to London where he worked as a trader in the city. My mum went to University in Liverpool and I believe I am a product of a one night stand. Not that Mum was loose or anything in fact think mum only had one other boyfriend. So my Aunty Millie told me.

"Aunty Millie?"

Yes, sadly Mum was in a coma for a lot of years so my Aunty Millie brought me up.

"So are your parents still alive?"

"Mum is dead as is Aunty Millie. My biological father I did find, but to be honest he was a total waste of space, so I never introduced myself. So, there is just me now."

"Aw Daniel, that's sad. So how did you end up in Paisley?"

"I was tracing my family tree. Came up for a week, loved the place and it's my home now."

They were so engrossed with each other they hadn't noticed the pub had emptied. The young bar man collecting glasses politely said they were closing.

Daniel and Anouska were like a pair of giggling school children as they stepped out onto the crisp fresh snow underfoot.

"I will walk you home. I live at the Green Tankard."

"Thought you might. A friend of mine said you were the manager."

"Oh, who was that?"

Anouska changed the subject which spooked Daniel a bit.

"Just up here Daniel," she said. They arrived at the apartment block. It was very swish for a student.

"Any chance of a coffee then?"

"Sorry Daniel, not on the first date."

She kissed him on the cheek and they exchanged mobile numbers. Anouska entered the entrance code and began climbing the stairs. She looked back and gave Daniel a little wave and a lovely smile.

Daniel felt like he was floating on air as he made his way back to The Green Tankard. Billy had asked him to work the following day, Christmas Day until 3.00pm. Then he said that they were having a Christmas dinner in the pub with some friends and a couple of locals were invited as well as Daniel.

The following morning Daniel woke early he felt like his life was changing. He had met a beautiful girl. The dreams had stopped and he wasn't thinking about things. Now he was just getting on with his life and ignoring all the doom and gloom Murdo had told him.

It was pleasant behind the bar. Everyone was buying him drinks and tipping him. The usual Slade record, Merry Christmas, was belting out of the juke box. To say the Scots are known for their Hogmanay celebration, they certainly were not shy about celebrating Christmas either. With the bar cleared by 3.00pm they settled down to Christmas dinner. There were seven people; Billy, Daniel, Mrs and Mrs Starkey, a couple of pensioners that came every year, Samantha Walters a barmaid at the pub and her husband Mike, and old Stan one of the regulars. The table was set for eight so Daniel asked Billy were they to wait for the eighth guest? Billy seemed a bit shaken at Daniel's question.

"Ugh no, I am sure he will be here at some time."

"Who is coming Billy?"

"Oh, you won't know him."

Daniel put some Christmas Carols on from Durham cathedral and left it playing quietly in the back ground. Just as Billy was passing out the carved turkey and goose, the door opened. To Daniel's shock in walked Leviathan Harkan. He was smiling and was dressed in one of those ridiculous Christmas jumpers with reindeers plastered all over it. Billy stood up, "Good to see you Mr Harkan we have saved a seat next to Daniel. Do you know each other Mr Harkan?"

"Yes, me and Daniel have made acquaintance, haven't we Daniel?"

Daniel could feel his annoyance boiling inside him as Harkan sat down next to him. Watching Harkan eat was disgusting to say the least as he continually brought his over large tongue out to mop up the spillages on his chin. Daniel thought it time to ask Billy how he knew Harkan.

"So, you and Mr Harkan are friends, Billy?"

"Well sort of."

"Don't be shy Billy," said Harkan. "We have known each other many years, haven't we Billy?"

Again Daniel could sense the nervousness in Billy's voice and the unease of the other guests. Daniel was determined to find out more later on that night. The Christmas pudding came out and Daniel felt physically sick watching Harkan mopping up the dribbles from the Christmas pudding cream with his tongue. Absolutely disgusting Daniel thought. He made and excuse to go to the toilet and he texted Anouska thanking her for a great Christmas Eve and tentatively asked her for a future date.

Daniel returned to find Harkan had left, and some of the others. There was just Billy and old Stan.

"I'll wash up Billy."

"I best be getting off then," said Stan seeing his chance to avoid the pots.

Billy cleared the table and Daniel started washing the pots. Once the table was cleared Billy came to dry what Daniel had washed.

"Didn't know you knew Harkan Billy."

Billy just mumbled something.

"He said you were old friends?"

Billy put the tea towel down.

"Go and get us to very large brandies please Daniel. We need to talk."

Daniel made his way behind the bar thinking he might get some answers here but also remembering he had promised himself he was putting all this behind him. With two large brandies in hand Billy and Daniel sat down at the kitchen table with the mountain of dirty pots behind them.

"What do you want to know Daniel?"

"I just wondered how you knew Harkan? I really don't like the man."

"Most people in a one mile radius of this pub are aware of Harkan and to be honest he isn't a man to cross. Daniel, you would be well advised to understand what I can tell you. People round he say he is Evil. He can appear and disappear at will."

"What do you mean?"

"Three years ago I needed money to buy this place. Old Stan told me to see Harkan, but he said don't default on any borrowed money. Anyway, nobody knows where Harkan lives but as if by magic he bumped into me and asked me how much I needed."

"How did he know?"

"That's just it Daniel. There was only me and Stan, and Stan had gone to his daughter's in Aberdeen two hours after our conversation."

"Did you ask Harkan how he knew?"

"No, I certainly didn't. I would not want to know the answer or feel the consequences. I told Harkan I needed ninety thousand pounds. He said no problem. We agreed a pay back of twelve hundred a month over seven years with the small amount of interest. I could not thank him enough. The deal was great I knew the pub would easily cover that. Everything went well until you arrived. Murdo came to see me and said Mr Harkan would like you employed at the Green Tankard. It wasn't a request it was more a command. Luckily I had a spare place so it turned out ok. Then a few months back Murdo came to me and said Harkan had said that he Murdo was going away for a short time. If you asked where he was, I was to make out I didn't know a Murdo."

Daniel swore, "who the hell does he think he is?"

"Daniel I really like you. All the locals like you but I dare not have the wrath of Harkan. Word out there is that Dick Garmin, a local hoodlum, crossed Harkan one night at the Bell Tavern the following morning he was found dead in an alley. The only thing the autopsy threw up was two dots on his neck. Now nobody questions Harkan or dares to cross him."

Daniel knew the symptoms as some of his guests at the wedding which was called off died the same way.

"Not sure I believe all this crap Billy."

"All I am saying is don't be foolish around him Daniel." They finished the pots and Daniel went to his room. The usual Christmas shows and films were on 'Only Fools and Horses', 'Emmerdale' and 'Tootsie' plus numerous others, none that Daniel wanted to watch. He lay on his bed trying to get Harkan out of his head he didn't want all this again he thought.

The following Boxing Day morning Daniel was working, but was off in the evening. In Paisley town centre they had like a traditional Christmas market. This had been a part of the Christmas celebration in Paisley for over two hundred years, so he was quite looking forward to going to that, albeit on his own.

Just gone two o'clock and Daniel got a text from Anouska. She asked him if he was going to the Christmas Market? If so she would see him by the William Wallace monument at 7.45pm. Daniel was ecstatic that she had sent him a message and he could not wait to meet her. With his shift finally finished Daniel went to his room and set his alarm for 6.00pm. He decided to take a nap, it had been a really busy day and he wanted to be fresh when he saw Anouska.

Daniel fell into a deep sleep and missed his alarm. He woke at 7.20pm. In blind panic he shaved, cutting himself in the rush, then showered and ironed a shirt and chinos. He dressed and grabbed his North Face quilted coat that Millie had bought him two years prior, and he rushed to the town centre. It was 7.55pm when he made his way through the crowds hoping that Anouska would still be there.

To Daniel's horror, under the statue of William Wallace he could see Anouska and Harkan chatting, both holding hot coffees.

"Ah Daniel, I was just saying to this pretty young lady how I knew you and that we had Christmas lunch together."

Daniel ignored Harkan's ramblings and leaned forward kissing Anouska on the cheek.

"Are you ok?" he whispered.

As he let go of Anouska he turned to Harkan but he had disappeared into thin air.

"What a nice man," Anouska said.

Daniel just smiled.

"He told me how he knew you and that you were special. I thought that was a nice thing to say Daniel."

Daniel never commented, he didn't want Anouska involved, but what was Harkan playing at? The crowd were in good spirits and everything seemed good. Daniel thought a new beautiful girlfriend was keeping his mind off all the nasty things that had blighted his life now.

Daniel and Anouska trod through the cobbled paths, with the snow now packed down by the crowds enjoying the market. The centre piece was a large ice rink.

"Come on Daniel, can you skate?"

"Not really Anouska, can you?"

"Of course I can. I am part Russian remember."

Anouska looked tremendous. She had beige leggings with small brown leather zip up boots. She had a brown three quarter coat trimmed with what looked like fox fur and a big fur Cossack hat. Daniel could not believe his luck. They paid six pounds each for half an hour on the ice. Anouska was graceful and had done one lap of the ice rink before Daniel had let go of the side.

"Come Daniel, hold my hand and be confident."

Poor Daniel was like Bambi on ice. He had gone down seven times before he decided maybe ice skating wasn't for him. So he took off his boots and watched the lovely Anouska as she twirled and skated like Jane Torvill.

After half an hour Anouska came off. They kissed and made their way to a small bar behind the ice rink. Although the bar wasn't that big, it may be held seventy people at a push. The landlord had put two tribute bands; on one was the Bay Roller

City, obviously a take on The Bay City Rollers, and the other band was The Four Props, a take on the Tamala Motown group, the Four Tops. First up was Bay Roller City singing Shang a Lang. They looked incredibly like the proper band with their tartan trousers and scarves. The floor cleared to make a dance floor and every age group from sixty to twenty danced. The group did a forty minute slot then the Four Props came on. This group was not what Daniel had expected. He had remembered Aunty Millie loved their music and in particular 'Reach Out I'll Be There'. She would play that song most Sundays while she was cooking dinner. The group consisted of two white guys and two black guys. Initially they each told a joke which was not expected, but then the lead singer started to sing 'Bernadette'. Daniel told Anouska about Millie and her favourite song and while he nipped to the toilet Anouska asked if they would sing it for him.

Daniel came back and the lead singer said he had a request from the lovely Anouska for her boyfriend Daniel Egan which they would now sing. He started sing 'Reach out I'll Be There'. Daniel could feel a lump in his throat. Anouska held him tight and a small tear trickled down his cheek.

"She was very special to you Daniel, wasn't she?"

The song finished and they decided to find a quieter pub and sit and talk. The Pig over the Moon was even smaller than the last pub and only had a few locals scattered around the room. They found a seat in the window and for the first time Anouska put her hand on Daniel's knee.

"I am so lucky to have met you Anouska."

"I think the same Daniel you are a lovely person. Have you been in a relationship since you have lived up here?"

Daniel didn't want to put Anouska off, but he also wanted to be honest from the start with no secrets.

"I was nearly married to Lee-Anne who I met when I first arrived in Paisley."

"When you say nearly what happened? Did she call it off?"

"It was weird, but half of the guests were struck down with an illness."

Daniel could not tell Anouska the real reason, he didn't want to spook her too much.

"Oh dear Daniel, that's terrible."

"Yes, well Lee-Anne said she couldn't get married with all the mayhem going on and I am afraid we drifted apart after that day."

He left the baby bit out as again he didn't want to alarm Anouska.

"What about you?"

She smiled her teeth glistening between her perfectly shaped lips.

"Well mine is a bit complicated. Also when I met you the other night my girlfriends had insisted I go out. I had broken up with my long-time boyfriend Simon Frith. We had met at University and lived together a couple of years, but he cheated on me with a junior doctor. As much as I loved him, I could not handle that so I called it a day. Being honest with you Daniel I still miss him. It's very early days and I don't want to rush things. Is that ok?"

"Hey of course. His loss is my gain," and he laughed.

It was close to closing time so Daniel helped Anouska with her coat and they walked back. It had started snowing again and Daniel felt happy with his lot. He had put Harkan to the back of his mind and was concentrating being happy. He kissed Anouska and she entered the password to her apartment and disappeared up the stairs.

Daniel arrived back at The Green Tankard and went straight to bed, turning down the offer of a brandy with Billy, who was sat by the fire. He said they had been really busy. Daniel was soon asleep. The last time he looked at his bedside clock it said 1.30pm.

The dreams had returned and Daniel felt he was actually there. He was in Brook Street and could see Harkan standing by the book shop beckoning him to go in. Inquisitively he wandered over.

"What's your game Harkan? Why do you keep getting involved in my life?"

Harkan laughed. His mouth was open and his teeth were green and his big tongue waggled over his mouth. Harkan went in the shop. A massive shock was about to greet Daniel. There standing against the book case was Aunty Millie, Lee-Anne and his best man Jack Holgarth who died at his ill-fated wedding. Daniel didn't know what to say. Millie looked younger as he remembered her when he was growing up. Lee-Anne on the other hand seemed to have aged. His biggest shock was Jack. He seemed crazed, his eyes were blood shot and he seemed to have the same type of tongue as Harkan. Nobody spoke.

"Aunty Millie," Daniel called out but there was no response. It was as if they were frozen in time. Daniel felt in his pocket and remembered the pebble that Murdo gave him.

"Am I dreaming Harkan?"

Harkan just laughed. On the dusty table that Daniel assumed had been used to read the books from the shelves, was a long sword like an Arabian sword. Harkan picked it up and handed it to Daniel.

"Your choice."

"My choice what?"

"Take their heads off Daniel."

"No," shouted Daniel and he threw the sword back on the table.

"Daniel, Daniel you ok?"

Daniel woke and could hear Billy banging on his apartment door. He gathered himself and went to the door.

"You alright lad? You woke me up with your scream."

"Oh, I'm sorry Billy, must have had a bad dream."

"Look at you lad you are soaked in sweat. Should have had that Brandy," Billy and Daniel laughed while Billy made his way back to his apartment.

Daniel made a cup of coffee and wrote down in his diary about the nightmare he had just had. This surely must just be a normal dream that people had but why now? Was it because he had been thinking about Aunty Millie with the song? And explaining about Lee-Anne and the wedding to Anouska, and obviously seeing Anouska at the start of the night talking with Harkan. He decided it was just that, and retired back to bed with no more dreaming.

The following day Anouska had phoned and asked if he would like to meet her for lunch at The Lavender Café in Holly Street. She was working but would nip out for lunch. Daniel said that was fine as he wasn't on until 3.00pm for his shift.

It was quite cold, although it had stopped snowing, as Daniel took the

ten minute walk to Lavender Café.
Anouska hadn't arrived, so he sat in
the window and ordered a coffee and
two menus ready for her arrival.
It was 1.20pm when she finally
arrived almost half an hour late.

"Oh, I am so sorry Daniel. We had
a bit of a panic on at work so I
couldn't just walk out."

"Hey, no problem, I enjoyed sitting
here people watching, although must
admit I thought I had been dumped."

"Don't be daft," Anouska said and
she playfully tapped Daniel on his
shoulder. With two coffees and two
Victoria sandwiches ready to
consume. They sat talking and
laughing, they seemed the perfect
couple. Daniel thought about telling
her about the latest dream but he just
wanted to forget about it and enjoy
this lovely lady's company.

Three months passed and Daniel had moved in with Anouska. It was early Spring when Daniel got home from his afternoon shift at the pub to find Anouska looking radiant.

"Daniel, I have some news for you," she said excitedly.

"Well I hope it's good like you have made me English sausage and chips instead of Haggis," and he laughed.

She playful tapped him.

"You are a fool Daniel. Hope you are ready for this."

"Ready for what?"

"You are going to be a daddy."

"What?"

Daniel's mouth dropped open.

"Really Anouska? That's great news, I love you so much."

"Oh, I am so pleased you are happy with the news."

"Of course I am happy why wouldn't I be?"

"Well it's a big responsibility Daniel."

"Look I am financially stable. I have never told you this, but I have two houses in London I rent out, and quite a large amount of money that I have been left by my mother and my Aunty Millie. We could sell those houses and buy a nice house with a garden for our child to enjoy and be safe. Let's start looking at the weekend and I will instruct the London estate agents to get the houses on the market."

"Oh, Daniel I don't deserve you."

"Ditto," he said.

With lunch over, Daniel dropped Anouska at work and decided to get the ball rolling on selling the houses in London.

As Daniel turned to walk down to the Green Tankard sitting on the low wall by the pub was Harkan. He had a yellow shirt on and a long blue trench coat with yellow trousers and white plimsolls.

Ah Daniel, how are you young man?"

"Why can't you just leave me alone?"

"I hear you have been asking about me Daniel. Now that isn't a wise thing to do."

"Harkan you don't frighten me. You are an evil man, why don't you say what you want from me then we can all get some peace."

Harkan laughed, his hideous tongue waggling about on his chin.

"Have a good day today Daniel," and with that he walked away.

Daniel felt frustration surging through him. He didn't want what he had come to Paisley. and specifically Grove, for anymore. He would be happy he thought with Anouska and the baby and a normal life. He was sick of the intrigue and the dreams. Daniel went in the Green Tankard shouted hello to Samantha Walters who was doing the early shift and headed up to his room.

At the top of the stairs Daniel could see Billy's apartment door open.

"Billy," he shouted but no answer. He thought he best shut his door but intrigue got the better of him and he went in to see if Billy was ok. On the floor there was a blood trail that went into the kitchen. Standing at the sink was Billy. His head was on the floor but he seemed alive until his head saw Daniel, and Billy's body dropped to the floor. Daniel immediately phoned 999. He was physically sick because he knew who had done this to Billy for talking with Daniel the night before.

The police arrived and took care of the body they sat Daniel down in his apartment. Samantha shut the pub and brought Daniel a large brandy to help with the shock. Daniel gave his statement but then Detective Webster noted Daniel had been at the scene of the murder of Hufton. Daniel now feared that he might get implicated in the murder of Billy. He decided to tell Detective Webster about seeing Harkan and what he had said.

"So this Mr Harkan, where does he live Daniel?"

"I don't know but he has a book shop on Brook Street."

"Really son? I don't think so."

Daniel knew he was in deep so said no more. Webster and his colleagues were smiling and looking at Daniel as if he was some sort of nut job. They took Daniel down to the station. After forty eight hours they told him they had found his DNA on

the knife that hacked off Billy's head
and they had also found three
thousand pounds of the pub takings in
a toilet cistern in his apartment.
Harkan had set him up and now he
had no Aunty Millie to help him.
Daniel sat with his head in his hands
then remembered the pebble. He had
nothing to lose he held the pebble and
wished he was with Anouska.

CHAPTER NINE

Everything went blank, and he found himself with his life gone forward two and half years. He was sitting in a beautiful garden with Anouska and their baby who they had called Jane Millie Egan after his mum and aunty. Anouska and Daniel were laughing and drinking Pimms. It was like nothing untoward had happened.

"So Daniel, to us and this beautiful house you bought, and to the success of the Green Tankard."

Daniel felt a little confused but could not explain to Anouska. He was determined not to bring her and the baby into this hell he was living.

"So, they finally arrested somebody for Billy's murder then Daniel?"

"Oh, I'm not sure."

"What do you mean you are not sure? You told me it was Old Stan, they even found the Christmas takings in his coat."

"Oh yes, sorry sweetheart, I was miles away."

The bloody pebble works he thought.

"Thank goodness your parents left you all that money, oh and Millie. It has set us up. I thought that Mr Harkan was kind to waiver the ninety thousand that Billy owed him, didn't you?"

"Yes, it was good of him."

"I saw him in Waitrose last week I forgot to tell you. He is a nice man, but a bit strange. He gave baby Jane a pebble. I took it off her in case she put it in her mouth."

"Don't accept presents off that man Anouska."

"Why?"

"Just don't, that's all and never invite him here. Am I clear?"

"Daniel why are you being so paranoid about Mr Harkan, after he has been so good to us?"

"I don't trust him Anouska. I will explain one day."

"Oh I give up, you grump. Come on Jane bath time," and she scooped the baby up leaving Daniel in the garden.

"Where did you put that pebble Anouska? I will get rid of it."

"I threw it away Daniel. I mean we don't want to accept a kindness from anyone do we?" she said sarcastically. If only she knew he thought. But that was it, he didn't want her to know. He had no need for a return journey with his pebble so still had three more times he could use it.

Apparently he now owned the Green Tankard and this beautiful house so he assumed the London houses had sold. He thought he would look at the bank account and try and wing it with Anouska.

"Anouska what is our password for the bank account."

"You are useless Daniel. We put everything with the Royal Bank of Scotland including the business accounts because you are always forgetting your password."

"I know sweetheart, just remind me."

"You said you wanted Cabhan. Not got a clue where that came from but you were insistent remember."

"Oh yeah of course. It was a name that stuck in my head from a book I read years ago."

Anouska carried on sorting Jane out and Daniel logged on. He was absolutely amazed at the account. Daniel had just over a million pounds in one account, which must have been the house sales in London. Then he had three hundred and twenty thousand in the business account which he assumed was money his mother and Aunty Millie left him. It looked like the pub was doing really well. Takings of over six thousand a week had been going in since the time gap of Billy's murder and Daniel finding himself with Anouska at this beautiful house.

Maybe things were good and Harkan would not bother them. If not, what are the options Daniel thought as he took a drink out of an ice-cold bottle of Corona lager?

"Are you going into work tonight Daniel?"

Daniel wasn't sure if he should or not.

"I'll see if they can cope, and if so shall we have a Chinese take away and watch a film?"

"That would be great Daniel, phone them quick."

Daniel phoned The Green Tankard and a voice on the end he didn't recognise "Green Tankard, Gabi Revell how can I help you?"

"Oh, hi Gabi, it's Daniel."

"Oh, hello Mr Egan, will you be in tonight?"

"How busy are you and who is on? I don't have the rota to hand," he said winging it again.

"Well I am behind the bar with Dirk Lumley. We have Jeff the chef and Sid the pot washer in the kitchen and my lass Kirsty waiting on."

"Great do you think you could cope if I took the night off?"

"Yes, no problem Mr Egan. I will make sure Jeff locks up."

"Thanks Gabi, see you tomorrow."

"Ok," and she hung up.

This was all weird Daniel thought, he didn't know her but she knew him. I suppose I should be grateful for the pebble but hopefully will never use it again he thought.

Daniel fetched the take away while Anouska finished putting Jane to bed and sorting a film for them to watch. Daniel got back and plated the Chinese up.

"There you go sweetheart, what film have you chosen?"

"It's a bit romantic."

"Oh, come on, can't we have a thriller or action movie?"

"No, it's my date night, so I have chosen 'The Slave of Claw Bay'. It's supposed to be brilliant, a girl at mothers and toddlers told me about it."

Daniel almost choked on his noodles.

"You ok Daniel?"

"Sorry, noodle went down the wrong way."

What if Cabhan comes up he thought.

The film was indeed about Cabhan, but not his Grandad Liam. He focused on Cabhan the slave, and how he rose out of deprivation to become a rich man. Daniel could not help thinking it was if somebody had read Liam's diaries. Was that possible he thought? But then it seems anything was possible in Daniel's world.
It wasn't until the film was almost over that Anouska clicked on to the name Cabhan.

"Are you being kind? Have you seen the film Daniel? The main character's name is our password you wanted."

"No, not seen it. Maybe I read the book at some time, but can't remember. How old is the film?"

"It says two and half years."

That was the exact time Daniel had lost with the pebble.
He hadn't dreamt anymore and he was hoping this wouldn't start things off. With the film finished they headed for bed. Anouska was reading 'The Wilmslow Boy' and Daniel was looking at his car magazine.

"Daniel," Anouska said, "could we clear all that junk out of the third bedroom? It would make a lovely room for Jane as she grows up. I looked the other day and I know the big brown box you said was your Grandad's and not to touch it, but why what's in it that is so secretive?"

He had his chance but then it will look like their whole relationship was built on lies.

"Nothing special, just something he left me, and some bits from Mum."

"Could they go in the loft?"

"Let me think about it."

"Well don't be stubborn about it because I want to do this, and if need be I will do it myself."

"I'll sort it next weekend, I promise," and he leaned forward and gave Anouska a kiss.

Daniel had no dream. Thank goodness he thought as he walked into work. He could see that there had been quite a few alterations. He saw a guy in chef whites so shouted, "morning."

From nowhere a portly guy with a beard popped his head round the door and said, "Morning Mr Egan. This is Tommy the new commis chef."

"Oh yes, nice to meet you Tommy."

Jeff whispered in Daniel's ear, "had to go up to seventeen thousand to get him but he is going to be very good."

"Ok well we need good staff," and Daniel headed to the bar thinking he won that one. The bar was empty other than a cleaner.

"Morning Mr Egan. How are Anouska and the bairn?" she said.

"Good thank you."

Daniel felt a bit bad with not knowing the cleaner's name.

"My Drew comes out of hospital today. Would be ok if I take a couple of mornings off just to bed him in."

"Yes, not a problem I am sure we will cope. Hope he gets better soon."

The cleaner looked at Daniel a bit puzzled and carried on with her chores. Next in was Gabi the barmaid. He luckily heard the chef shout her name when she came in and she answered, "morning Jeff" as she was hanging her coat up. Gabi was in her mid-thirties, a typical Scottish barmaid who clearly had a hard life.

"There you go love, we had a bit of a collection last night for Drew. I know it's not a lot what have they said," she said to the cleaner.

"He will probably last a week but he wanted to come and be in his home surroundings. He has got all his estate in order."

Daniel stood listening to this and now realised why the cleaner looked at him puzzled when he had said he hoped her husband would get better soon. At least he got most things right he thought. By lunchtime the bar and eating areas were very busy. He had certainly turned the Green Tankard round, he didn't know how, just knew he had. Daniel took time to look at the rota and noticed that the following night somebody called Lee-Anne was working in the bar. He went cold. Had he set Lee-Anne on and not known? Daniel couldn't ask anyone so he decided he would help on the bar the following night. As he put his name down on the rota Jeff walked in and saw him.

"She is a tidy piece, that one Mr Egan. All the lads are trying there and she has only done three shifts so far."

Daniel smiled. So, if it was indeed Lee-Anne, she hadn't been there long.

With the pub busy Daniel went back to look at the invoicing. It was immaculate so Daniel knew it wasn't his work. On a sticky note on the computer screen somebody had put 'message to myself must do the VAT on Friday' and then she had put 'No ducking it Karen'! So, he must have an office girl called Karen. He checked the personnel file first to see Lee-Anne's file but there was nothing on her, but there was a Karen Frome it simply said administration.

With Friday being the next day he decided to tell Anouska he was working right through as he wanted to meet Karen and also to see if it was really Lee-Anne working the bar. Friday soon came and Daniel found himself putting aftershave on and some nice clothes for work because of meeting with the mysterious Lee-Anne.

"Blimey Egan, if I didn't know better, I would guess you were on the pull," and Anouska laughed.

"What with the most gorgeous woman in the world as my partner. I don't think so do you?"

"Stranger things have happened Mr Egan," and she laughed and picked Jane out of her chair to wave Daniel off. He felt somewhat guilty. She was right. What was he going to do if it was Lee-Anne? Why be bothered, she walked out on him? Daniel arrived at work. The kitchen staff were in full flow. They seemed a happy bunch and Jeff was certainly very good. He walked down the corridor to what was now the office. In Billy's time it was a sitting room. Perched at her desk was Karen. Karen was slim maybe late twenties, dressed in all black, with the most dazzling blue eyes. Daniel just played daft.

"Morning Karen."

"Morning Daniel."

She was the first of his employees to call him by his Christian name.

"How are you today?"

"Bit of a headache. I went out with my next-door neighbour last night to see The Clash. They were playing at the Paisley Hippodrome. It has just reopened it and I guess we had too many sherbets, and now I have this bloody VAT to do, so please don't make too much noise."

"I won't, I promise."

That went well he thought. He looked at his watch, it was now 10.50am. The mysterious Lee-Anne was due on at 11.00am. Spot on 11.00am he heard Jeff say, "Morning Lee-Anne, would you like some breakfast?"

She replied that she had to watch her figure.

"Looks good from where I am standing," Jeff said. Daniel was too far away to hear Lee-Anne's voice clearly, so he straightened himself and headed to the bar. The blonde-haired girl was bent down bottling up.

She jumped, "You startled me!" It was Lee-Anne but it was like she didn't know him.

"Can you spare a minute?"

"Yes, if you wish."

Daniel made two coffees and told Lee-Anne to sit at the far end of the room. He sat down feeling nervous.

"What are you doing here Lee-Anne? Where have you been?"

"You told me you had moved on and I wasn't to call you. It was like you were ashamed of me. You would not listen to my side of the story would you?"

Daniel apologised, and told Lee-Anne what had happened to Billy, and how he got away, and about Anouska and baby Jane. Lee-Anne in return told Daniel her story.

"You are not going to like this Daniel but I had to leave London. Millie had been possessed."

"Don't be silly Lee-Anne."

"Believe what you will, but the shaking was a part of it. Harkan told me. He also told me lots of other things, but said if I repeated them to you or anyone I was dead."

"Don't tell me Lee-Anne. I think that's why Billy was murdered."

"Look this is too much to take in. Are you free for a coffee tomorrow?"

"Are you sure Daniel? You are out of this. Do you really want to chance losing Anouska and the baby?"

"That's my decision but we can't go local. Drive out to Reverence, there is a small coffee shop in the village called Violets Delicious Bake."

"Ok, well I guess we better get doing some work."

Lee-Anne and Daniel spent the rest of the day politely avoiding each other.

Daniel arrived home at almost midnight. He pulled into his drive and noticed that the living room light was on which must have meant Anouska must have stayed up, which she never did.

Daniel put his key in the door and unlocked it he shouted, "Anouska," but could hear crying coming from the living room. Daniel entered the room. Anouska was sat wiping tears from her eyes. On the floor was an empty envelope and on the coffee table was an A4 sheet with writing on it.

"Why could you not be honest with me Daniel?"

"What are you on about?"

Anouska threw the paper at him. Daniel sat on the arm of the leather chair across from Anouska and began reading.

'Dearest Anouska

It is with some concern for you and your child that I write this letter in some haste.

It is clear that you are blissfully unaware you share you lives with a murderer and a most evil man.

GROVE

Daniel Egan murdered a Mr Hufton some years ago, simply because he wrote a few books about the supposed malevolent place called Grove, which I would suggest he has never mentioned to you? Since he took over the Green Tankard everybody now knows he killed poor harmless Billy then framed Old Stan for his murder. Stan could not have killed a fly, Anouska.

I write you this letter knowing if Daniel Egan was to find I have penned these allegations, then I would surely be murdered just like Mr Hufton and poor Old Stan.

I take no pleasure in writing this and it is with a heavy heart. Take heed my dear Daniel Egan is evil and you will do well to leave Paisley with some haste and never return.

Yours Mr Apollyon'

Daniel sat for a minute with the room in total silence and Anouska staring at him in disbelief.

"So, what have you got to say Daniel?"

"Look, I have had a long day Anouska, this is just rubbish."

"If you are not prepared to talk to me, I am taking Jane and we are going away."

"Look Anouska, I am trying to protect you."

"From what Daniel, your evil self?"

"I have heard enough."

"Please wait Anouska."

"Then tell me the truth."

"Ok but this is going to sound weird. I came to Paisley and specifically the village of Grove because of some diaries I was left by my mother."

"Is that what is in a sealed box in the loft?"

"Yes, but I never wanted you to read them, because first of all it sounds weird, and secondly the chilling message I was given at Grove church. I think the best thing would be for you to read the diaries including mine tomorrow while I am at work, then I can try and explain this mess. I need to go to bed Anouska. You should know I would never hurt you or Jane."

Anouska didn't know what to think but for now was contented with Daniel's explanation.

The following morning Daniel got the diaries from the loft, including his diary that he kept in the garage hidden away. He put them on the kitchen table and left a note for Anouska to say he would be home about 8.00pm.

He arrived at The Green Tankard mindful he was seeing Lee-Anne in the village of Reverence a few miles out of Paisley at lunchtime. Jeff, the chef, was his usual happy self and shouted good morning to Daniel as he waked down to his office to sort rotas and the wages. Daniel was finding it hard to concentrate. He was trying to figure out who had written the letter. Daniel's only thought was Harkan but it didn't seem his style. So, who the hell was Mr Apollyon? He played with the name to see if it was an anagram or something but no joy.

Daniel left at 12.15pm. Lee-Anne had texted to say she would be there in twenty minutes. He could have done without this with the letter and things with Anouska, but Lee-Anne had said she had something to tell him.

 Daniel arrived at the café in the small village of Reverence and parked in the small car park. He walked into the Victorian styled café and was shown to a window seat. Lee-Anne hadn't arrived, but just as he was explaining to the waitress she appeared.

"Sorry Daniel my car is playing up and wouldn't start at first."

"No problem, I have only just got here myself."

The waitress came over dressed in all black with a lacy neck and sleeves.

"Good afternoon Sir and Madam," she said.

"Could I take your order?"

"What would you like Lee-Anne?"

"Could I have a tea and a tuna crunch baguette with the small salad please?"

"For you Sir?"

"I will also have the tea and may I have the steak and Dijon mustard baguette?"

"It will be with you shortly," said the waitress and she left.

Both Daniel and Lee-Anne were nervous as they both tried to speak at the same time.

"You first Lee-Anne."

"Ok Daniel, but I have a feeling what I tell you will cost me my life."

"What, you think Harkan will kill you?"

"I know he is waiting to kill you and your family."

"What do you mean?"

"When I left you in London there was a reason?"

"What do you mean?"

"Well that afternoon Millie was feeling a bit under the weather so I went for a walk. I walked for about three miles and came across a beautiful park. I think it was called

Fairy Dell or something like that. I sat for a minute on a park bench and from nowhere Harkan appeared. I was frightened Daniel I couldn't see anybody in the park. He told me that Millie was shaking because she was one of them and her mind and body had been taken from her. He told me to leave and not to explain anything to you. He also told me at the wedding that he murdered those people because they could never be one of them."

"What is one of them Lee-Anne?"

"I don't know, but I do know he meant what he said. He also laughed. He said you had been sent to eradicate them but you had so far failed all the tests and would soon be one of them."

"What tests? What is he on about?"

"He said your family had fought this over many centuries but your ancestor Dermot Egan was valiant and was a leader amongst men.

"This guy is a nut job Lee-Anne."

"Don't underestimate him Daniel, Anouska and your child are in grave danger."

"She received a letter yesterday Lee-Anne telling her about the diaries and all those things I never told her, because I didn't want her involved. I was convinced you left me because of all this and I thought if I shielded her from it we would be fine."

"Do you still have dreams Daniel?"

"Hardly ever."

Daniel was thinking should he tell her about the shiny pebble. She had been open with him at the risk of her life. Maybe he owed it to her to give her the pebble in case Harkan did try to kill her.

"I was given this stone. I actually call it a pebble because it looks more like a pebble than a stone."

Daniel produced it and told Lee-Anne it would transport her wherever she wished, which could take her out of Harkan's reach. Now she had told him her story you take it.

"I can't do that Daniel."

"Look, it helped me once and you are in danger. I can look after myself, Lee-Anne. Just hold the pebble sweetheart and wish, and thank you for trying to warn me. I will always be grateful." The waitress arrived with the tea and food. Lee-Anne took a drink of her tea thanked Daniel she then closed her eyes and within seconds she had gone and the pebble with her. Daniel finished his baguette and tea and called the waitress over to pay her.

"I am sorry Sir has your friend left? Was the food not to her liking?"

"No, she just ran out of time."

"Oh well I am sorry I won't charge you for your friend's tea and food."

Daniel decided not to disagree as it was easier than trying to explain. He thanked the girl, left her a tip and headed back to work. He just wanted to make sure everything was ok, and decided he would leave at six instead of eight like he had told Anouska. It was playing on his mind what Lee-Anne had said.

It was soon six and everything was ok at the pub so Daniel left. On the way back he bought Anouska some flowers from the garage, not ideal but at least it was a gesture.

He arrived home and all the lights were on. Anouska's car wasn't in the garage, and the house was empty except for a letter he found on the kitchen table with all the diaries.

GROVE

Daniel sat and read the letter.

'Dear Daniel

I thought we had the perfect relationship and when Jane came along that cemented everything. How wrong was I? You have lied to me about so many things including actually standing at the altar to be married. How could you do that to me? I have always been honest and open with you. Those stupid diaries, I can see now that you are obsessed with them and it took over your life.

I know this must be hard for you to take but I have to protect Jane from all this. I can't have this ruining her life. I am still getting my head round the diaries.

You won't ever see me or Jane again. I really do hope you can walk away from this awful fascination you have with the past.

    Goodbye Daniel

    Anouska.'

CHAPTER TEN

Daniel sat with his head in his hands feeling desperate and lonely. The following morning after very little sleep he made his way into work. He had texted and called Anouska over three hundred times but she wasn't going to answer. He had to realise that she was gone and to move on. Hopefully one day she would come back with Jane.

Jeff tried to cheer him up when he arrived at work. Daniel said they had a blazing row and she had walked out. He wasn't going to tell anyone the real reasons.

It was late afternoon and Daniel was doing the bar when Sky News reported a bad accident in Loch Filey, some hundred and thirty miles from

Paisley. At first Daniel was only half listening but they said the make of the car and that a woman was driving and a little girl was in a baby seat. An articulated lorry had swerved and hit them. The new report said both the woman as yet unidentified and the little girl were decapitated on impact. Daniel then saw the registration which was 'ANO 5SKA'. Daniel had bought it her for Christmas. His heart sank.

"Jeff where is Loch Filey? How do I get there?

"Oh, there is a famous distillery there. Put that in your sat nav it will take you there, it's only a small village. Why Daniel?"

"I can't tell you. Look after this place. I may not be in for a few days. I will sort you a bonus Jeff."

"Ok Daniel, no problem."

Daniel grabbed his coat and drove like a mad man. All the way he was shaking hoping it was all a mistake.

Two hours later he drove in to the village. The road had been cleared, there was just one police car with a constable removing incident tape from the scene. Daniel stopped and asked the constable if he could give him an update. He told Daniel that the car was at Andrew's garage in the village. The woman and the child died at the scene. Daniel said he thought it was Anouska and his child. The policemen stopped for a minute.

"Oh, I am so sorry. If that is the case follow me to the station and you will be able to identify their belongings. What's your name Sir?"

"Daniel Egan."

"Follow me then, Mr Egan."

They passed Andrew's garage. It was Anouska's car which was crushed. He could just see her personalised number plate hanging down from the wreckage, Tears rolled down his cheek as the police man showed him into the station and explained to the desk sergeant who he was.

"Take a seat Sir and I will get somebody out to see you."

A few minutes passed and a Detective came out.

"Mr Egan," and he offered his hand to shake.

"DI Newey, follow me Sir."

Daniel was shown into a room and given a coffee with plenty of sugar in it for the shock. He identified the personal belongings of both Anouska and Jane.

"Sir this is really not the right time. We will understand if you wish to take a couple of days before identifying the bodies, but both bodies are in the morgue."

"No, I would sooner get this over with."

The mortician had done his best to make the heads seemed connected. Daniel looked at little Jane and almost fainted then he moved to Anouska. He started crying and shaking, and it was then he noticed the two red dots on Anouska's neck.

"Harkan, it's Harkan's doing."

"Sir calm, down what do you mean?"

Daniel collected himself. "Sorry nothing."

"No worries, this must be dreadful for you."

"The bodies will be released for collection in two day's time. If you wish to arrange with a funeral director Mr Egan."

Daniel decided to stay in Loch Filey until the bodies were released. He contacted a funeral director in Paisley and the local church of St Anne's. Anouska had always said that one day they would be married there.

Daniel knew drinking wasn't the answer, but it deadened the hurt and the thoughts of revenge on Harkan. He sat in the small village pub and slowly drowned his sorrow before climbing to bed.

Daniel was soon asleep and for the first time in a long time he started dreaming.

He felt cold and found himself walking towards something in the distance, but the snow and icy weather made it impossible to see what he was walking towards. In the distance he could see a shadowy figure beckoning him. Daniel got closer and the figure looked seven feet tall it was dressed in brown sack cloth with a hood. Daniel couldn't see the face.

The figure spoke, "It's close to choice time Daniel. Follow us and all will be well. Follow the wrong sect and damnation will follow you."

"Who are you?"

"The figure threw back his hood to reveal a grotesque face covered in scales with bulging eyes, all blood shot. Daniel reeled back.

"Why are you doing this to me?"

"You know why Daniel, you were chosen weren't you? You will be contacted very soon by our representative on earth. You would do well to follow his instructions."

The figure turned and disappeared into the distance.

Daniel woke almost immediately he was drenched in sweat and had a terrible headache. He looked at the clock it said 8.20pm two days later.

Had he been asleep for over two days?

Daniel went downstairs and the landlord asked him if he was ok.

"I was a little worried about you Mr Egan. A Mr Timolan, funeral director asked me to ask you to call him urgently."

"Ok thank you. I will be checking out in the morning."

Daniel called Timolan and he said they were picking the bodies up in the morning and they would be at his Chapel of Rest until the funeral one week later at St Anne's. He said that Daniel needed to see the vicar for what he would like at the service. Daniel thanked Timolan and said he would be back in Paisley the following day. Daniel felt empty he had cried and cried. He had that awful dream and knew at some point his time was coming, but he didn't know why?

Everyone at the Green Tankard was supportive. They told him Lee-Anne appeared to have left without giving notice. Daniel said not to worry there were plenty of people wanting bar work.

Daniel spoke with the vicar of St Anne's, Reverend Markham, a small portly man with glasses. The funeral was arranged for 10.00am the following day, with the vicar now aware of the order of service.

Daniel decided to hold the wake at The Green Tankard. All the staff wanted to go to the funeral so Jeff said he would stay and get things ready for when they returned.

The day of the funeral arrived. Daniel felt empty inside as the funeral car arrived to pick him up for the Church. Although only five minutes, the drive felt like an eternity. This was the day he would be burying his beautiful Anouska and his little girl. If only he could find the person responsible for the letter. Daniel tried to not have negative thoughts on the already very difficult day.

The congregation consisted of eight staff from the pub. A neighbour Anouska had made friends with, and four strange looking people who were dressed in all black; two men and two women. They stood at the back and were all the same height and were the same stature. Daniel was unsure who they were.

"Ladies and Gentlemen," said the vicar. "We are gathered here today to celebrate the life of Anouska Deblinker Duxbury and Jane Millie Egan. Daniel has told me what a stunningly beautiful girl she was, and how their life was complete on the arrival of their daughter Jane Millie, named after Daniel's mum and aunty.

Daniel and Anouska met a few years ago and it was love at first sight he told me. The song that the coffin came into church was called 'When I was Your Man'. The vicar said, "This is a song very close to Daniel's heart and he tells me even more so as he says his goodbyes. It was the song playing in the background when he noticed her all those years ago."

"If you could all please stand for our first hymn 'Morning Has Broken'". The small congregation tried desperately hard as did the vicar to sing the song, but the effect was minimal on the volume.

"Please be seated," said the vicar. "I will now read you a passage from the bible John.14.1-6
Jesus said do not let your hearts be troubled.
Trust in God; trust also in me
In my Father's house are many rooms; if it were not so, I would have told you. I am going there to prepare a place for you. And if I go to prepare a place for you, I will come back and take you to be with me that you may also be where I am. You know the place to where I am. You know the place to where I am going. Thomas said to him, Lord we don't know where you are going so how can we know the way?Jesus answered, I am the way the truth and the life. No one comes to the Father except through

me."

Daniel could hear sniggering at the back of the church. In fact everyone could hear it and they turned around in unison to see who had such bad manners. It appeared to come from the four strangers. They showed no embarrassment at the congregation looking at them. They just stared straight ahead. Daniel decided after the funeral he was going to give them a piece if his mind.

The vicar announced the next hymn 'The Day Though Gavest Lord is Ended'. Again, the congregation valiantly tried to sound like it was a full church. All through the hymn Daniels eyes were fixed on Anouska's coffin and his little girls. All his dreams were there in front of him gone forever.

GROVE

The vicar said Daniel would now like to say a few words. Daniel made his way to the pulpit tears rolling down his cheek. He straightened his tie cleared his throat and began his speech.

"Today is the worst day of my life. We had so many plans together and when Jane Millie was born we were complete. Anouska was an incredible mother and partner. She was very patient, understanding and honest. Anouska cared for everyone, always seeing the good side of everyone, never wishing to judge people. She was loved by everyone she met. She had the looks of a film star and the heart of a saint. My beautiful Anouska."

Daniel had to stop to compose himself.

GROVE

"To lose Anouska and to lose my Jane at the same time is a blow, but I know there is a higher being with a plan, and I know we will be reunited one day as family once more. I just want to read a short poem."

"So go and run free. Dance around the golden clouds. For the lord has chosen them to be with him. We should feel nothing but proud although he has taken them from us.

Our pain a lifetime will last their memory will never escape us. Make us glad for the time we did have. Each precious moment you both gave us shall never ever be forgotten. Go and run free with the Angels my lovely girls. My heart is broken but one day we will be together again"

Daniel stepped down from the pulpit still annoyed by the ignorance of the

four people at the back, but they had
gone.

The vicar stood up as the funeral
bearers picked up the coffin.

"Daniel has asked that we play this
song as the coffins of Anouska and
Jane are taken on their final journey.
Daniel has asked me to tell you that
there are refreshments at The Green
Tankard public house in Paisley after
the burial."

As they carried the coffin out to the
song 'Photograph' most people were
wiping tears form their eyes. The
whole of the congregation attended
the grave side.

As Daniel was stooping to put some
soil on the coffins out of the corner of
his eye he saw Harkan in a bright red
suit with white shirt and dickie-bow.

GROVE

He cocked his hat but then simply disappeared. Daniel knew he had to confront this man, he had taken everything off him. On the way back to the Green Tankard he knew he had to get this day over, then he was determined to seek out Harkan. In his current state of mind he wanted to kill him, as he saw all the things that had gone wrong were down to Harkan.

The Green Tankard was quite busy. Everyone was talking about the two men and two women that were at the back of the church through the service, and how ignorant they were. But nobody seemed to know who they were or where they came from.

Jeff had laid out a very nice spread for about thirty people. Only maybe twenty actually were at the wake so there was plenty to go round.

GROVE

By 8.00pm most people had gone and just the normal trade was coming in.

"It's been a long day Jeff, thank you for everything you do. Would you mind if I called it a day?"

"Of course not Daniel, try and get some rest mate."

"Not sure I can but I will try Jeff, and thanks again."

Daniel put his coat on. He had hardly had anything to drink so he drove home. Once inside he sat on the leather settee with a picture of Anouska and Jane and a large whisky.

How could this be happening to him he thought? All he wanted was a normal life and he thought he had it. He got his laptop and started putting in different spellings for Apollyon, the man who had signed the letter. He was then struck on the importance of the meaning he typed in on his laptop.

Apollyon was a Greek word for Devil, things started to fall into place. When the old lady said Daniel had come to save the human race, it was to save it from the Devil. Now all he had to do was find out who represented the Devil.

A couple of months went by and Daniel was having no luck in finding the person that sent the letter that created the deaths of Anouska and Jane. He tried many time to find Harkan but the shop was shut up and he would spend every waking minute of his spare time wandering the streets of Paisley looking for him.

One night while he was watching TV he heard something moving in the kitchen. Fearing for his life he picked up a brass candle stick and quietly headed to the kitchen. To his total surprise Lee-Anne was standing there.

"What the hell are you doing here?"

"I couldn't stay away any longer Daniel. I am so sorry for what happened to Anouska and Jane."

"But Lee-Anne I gave you a get out plan and now you are back that means the pebble has only one go left. If you go again you will be stuck in that time warp."

"I'm not going again Daniel. I want you to go."

"Why would I go? I have unfinished business with the person that wrote the letter and Harkan. I'm going nowhere."

"Daniel if you don't go and you don't join them, then you will die and the rest of humanity will suffer forever."

"Lee-Anne how do you know so much about this?"

"I have been evil and I can see evil in people. I know your aunty Millie became evil through association with you. She became possessed."

"No Aunty Millie was the sweetest person ever. She died because she tried to fight it once she was possessed."

"Daniel, you are good but they will twist things and make you think you are evil. You have to use the pebble to get away. I should never have let you help me or you would have three chances. Now you only have one. I am doomed they will come for me. They consider you a top prize because of your ancestors and mainly Dermot Egan."

"Who is Harkan and who wrote that letter Lee-Anne?"

"I wrote the letter."

Daniel stood flabbergasted.

"Why would you do that?"

"For you and your family. I thought if I could get Anouska and the child away from you they would leave them alone and concentrate on you. I thought that is what you would have wanted."

"When you said you were evil, what did you mean by that?"

"Sit down Daniel and I will tell you everything as there is no hope for me now."

"Look Lee-Anne, I am sure you did what you did for the best of reasons, and if by not telling me what you are about to tell me saves your life then don't tell me."

"It is over for me Daniel so just listen."

"I was born in 1591 in a village called Lothan near Suffolk. My mother was a sickly woman and almost died in childbirth. She eventually did die when my brother was still-born in 1601. I was only nine when I had to cook, wash and do the chores of a wife for my father who worked in the forest. He was a nasty brute of a man, always drunk and fighting. When I reached the age of fifteen he came home one night blind drunk, and he didn't like the food I had made so he hit me repeatedly. I cried and cried. Then it was if something possessed me, and I found strength and I choked him with my bare hands."

Believe me Daniel there were and are such things as witches. Just that as people have become educated, they have swept it under the carpet. Because I was a pretty young thing at that time, they only assumed old women with crooked noses, hair on their top lip or a cat was a sure sign of a witch. I had an evil way with me by now and found I could just look at somebody and they would be struck down with illness."

"So, what are you saying? You were born in 1591 and have lived all this time?"

"No what happened was I lived until I was seventy three. I was reborn to those ghastly parents. I can't explain but three years before I met you I resurfaced in Paisley. Why Paisley? I didn't know until you arrived then things began to fall into place."

"Just let me go back to the year of 1611. I was now established as an evil person and would quite often have awful dreams about things I had to do. I can vividly remember falling out with a Mrs Sarah Oldfield who was a kindly lady. But I put it about that I had seen her in the woods at night collecting plants with her ginger tom cat. I said she had seen me once and told me if I ever uttered a word about what she was doing she would put a spell on me for eternity. All lies of course. The way they got women to say they were witches was through torture and because I had made the accusations I was allowed to torture her for her confession."

"Sarah Oldfield was very resilient first. With the court watching I administered the first punishment which was the 'Pilnie –winks' which were a kind of crude thumb screw. She screamed but would not say she was a witch. She even said the poor girl, meaning me, was mistaken. The torture went on for two days. The court then instructed me to use the 'Caspie Claws', which were leg irons heated on a brazier then clamped to the leg of the witch. She finally cracked screaming forgiveness. The court ordered her to be burnt at the stake and her house be razed to the ground. In effect leaving her husband and four children homeless."

"This is unbelievable."

"I would say almost everyone that I ever saw that was hung or burnt at the stake were not witches. The witches that I knew were far too clever to be caught. "

"In 1639 I was still practising this evil but I didn't know why. It was like I was driven to do it. Margaret Staith was an unlikely victim. She was wife of the Lord of the Manor and her husband put the rents up to raise taxes for Charles I, for an army to fight the Scottish Covenanters. I saw a chance to set his wife up, so I did. She was out riding one day so I pulled her off her horse in the forest. I then cast a spell on her which made her walk through the village warning anyone who was near her that she would put a spell on them. Everyone was shocked but the one person I wanted her to threaten was the witch hunter who was at the village at the time. John Legley was a fearsome man and needed little excuse to burn a woman at the stake. Because of the amount of witnesses that came forward, no trial was needed. She was burnt at the stake with her husband pleading for mercy."

"Needless to say, the Great Hall was ransacked and razed to the ground. Lord Staith hung himself a year later a broken man."

"Wow, so why are you telling me all this now?"

"Because when I resurfaced here in Paisley I was a normal girl, but after I read the dairies and about Grove my evilness started coming back. I don't have powers now but until your act of kindness with the pebble I would never have been free from them. I am now, they can't hurt me because of the kindness at your cost you showed me. You were the special one. What I am telling you is they have to make sure you join them or they could easily be finished. So, I want you to take the pebble and disappear where they won't find you."

"I'm sorry Lee-Anne but I can't run. I will find Harkan someday and then I will kill him."

"But that's it Daniel, you won't and if you do then you will join them as evil. So, you see Daniel they are making you think evil, please go far away."

Lee-Anne handed Daniel the stone.

"Lee-Anne, I have to ask you about our baby what happened. Was that Harkan?"

"Yes, the day he came to the apartment and touched my baby lump. He did kill our baby, he could not chance another you, in case he could not turn you. Whichever way this goes he wins Daniel."

"We will see Lee-Anne. Are you coming back to work?"

"If you don't mind."

"Of course I don't mind. I am pleased you have been honest with me."

Lee-Anne left and Daniel went to bed, his mind in a total mess.

CHAPTER ELEVEN

Nothing happened for over a year. No sign of Harkan, no dreams and Daniel and Lee-Anne had slowly rekindled their relationship. They were both trying to put their past behind them.

It was early June when a man and woman came in the pub they said they were from the Grove restoration project and could they leave a poster about an open day they were having to raise funds. They also asked if they could leave a collection tin.

Daniel didn't know what to say when the woman started giving him and history lesson on Grove. Lee-Anne could see Daniel was a little apprehensive. She stood talking for almost half an hour trying to get Daniel to provide a bar at the event.

Eventually Daniel agreed and the women left happy.

"Do you think that's wise Daniel?"

"Well I suppose not, but we can't keep living our lives on ifs, buts and maybes, can we?"

Lee-Anne didn't answer she knew it could well be a costly mistake for both of them.

The event at Grove came around and Daniel pushed the boat out with a big bar and awnings advertising the Green Tankard. The village looked incredible. The Grove Society had really gone to town as they were expecting visitors from all over the world. On what had been the village green they had an old fashioned fun fair with swing boats, hook a duck and dodgems.

There were plenty of food stalls selling everything from hot pork cobs to fish and chips. It didn't seem like the dark foreboding place Daniel had seen the first time he arrived at the Church. Even the church had been opened for visitors. There were talks inside the church on the history of Grove and how it had such a dramatic demise in its fortunes.

By 3.30pm Daniel had a relief on the bar, and Lee-Anne was working as well, so he decided to have a wander round. The society had got its members to dress up in the clothes of the era. Daniel felt quite spooked having travelled back in time and actually been there and seen how they lived.

Some research had been done and where each house and the pub stood small name plates were on sticks pushed into the ground. The pub had William Brewster as the landlord but it just said died mysteriously. The next name plate said Malky McAndrew and family. Malky died after an argument in a pub somewhere near Grove he supposedly stuck up for Ellie Fairbury a serving wench. It is said he died for crossing the devil. There were a few name plates missing, then the next one shocked Daniel to the core of his being. Leviathan Harkan and his family lived here. He was a preacher man and a good man until one day he went mad with fever and cut off the heads of his four children and poor wife. It was said he was from that day possessed by Evil. Daniel was getting a picture of what all this meant. Harkan lived at the time of Dermot Egan which he hadn't realised. Daniel followed the small map that the society had put together. Eventually he found the plaque he had been looking for. Dermot Egan lived here with his family an Irish Immigrant. He came to Grove looking for work in the mines. Egan didn't mix well. He was a nasty giant of a man. The whole village was frightened of him and his children. If he walked down the dusty street people would go in their houses for fear of retribution from the man.

It was said that Egan was in bed with the Devil and during the harsh winter that saw so many of the village starve Egan always had food and fuel for the fire. He didn't work and would spend his time in the taverns where people were so frightened off him they would not charge for his ale.

Great, Daniel thought, trust me to have the nasty ancestor. A lady in her mid forties came and stood next to him.

"You are Daniel Egan of The Green Tankard pub, aren't you?"

"Yes, why? Daniel said.

"Nothing, it's just I do a lot of research for the society and me and my hubby just had a pleasant glass of your fine beer at your stand. I over-heard somebody say your name so I put two and two together and came looking for you."

"So are you related to the legend, if I may call him that. of Dermot Egan?"

Daniel thought for a few seconds.

"Yes, I am unfortunately. I guess if you believe all that mumbo jumbo."

"Surprisingly Mr Egan, we have good records for Grove because not far away was a Friary. Monk Gellycombe, a learned monk, kept precise records. He would pay for any gossip with jars of honey, then he would research the truth before writing it all down."

"How do you know all this?"

"Well I am a professional researcher and was asked initially by the society to help, but now I am part of the society."

"If you are free one night I would like to discuss Grove with you over a meal perhaps."

"Thank you that would be nice could we say this Friday say 8.00pm."

"Yes, where would you like to eat?"

"There is an Argentinean restaurant in Paisley, it's called Kempes. I will book a table for three shall I?"

"Friday is fine for me but Gordon my husband has to go back to Edinburgh on Wednesday so just book the table for us two. Would your wife not like to join us Mr Egan?"

"No, I am afraid not I'm not married."

"Oh ok, well my name is Amanda Cook. I am a lecturer at Edinburgh University and I look forward to our meal and hopefully being able to enlighten you on your ancestors of Grove."

Amanda Cook left Daniel still looking at the ruins of his ancestor's house. Next stop which was the most daunting, was to go to St Matthews Church. The society had a vicar dressed in the clothes of the time and children dressed as street urchins. They had put flowers leading up to the church which brightened it up somewhat, and made it less eerie. Daniel decided to take a look at the gravestones which he had never done. He found William Brewster's and some other names but he could not find Dermot Egan's or Leviathan Harkan. He thought how odd that was, and he made a mental note to ask Amanda Cook about this on Friday.

He decided to go inside the church. He could see a woman in a brown dress with a white headscarf kneeling down with her hands clasped praying. Daniel passed her and sat a few pews to the right. He prayed as he always had been told to do by Millie when he first went in a church. When he had finished praying he got up to take a look round and saw the face of the lady in the white headscarf.

"Anouska, Anouska." The lady turned to walk away. Daniel could see it was Anouska. He followed but she simply appeared to walk through the church wall. Daniel slumped back in a pew exhausted from all the information and tragedy that had gone on in his life. He had seen his beautiful Anouska was his mind playing tricks?

He ran outside but she was nowhere to be seen.

GROVE

"You ok Sir?" said the man dressed as the vicar.

"Oh eh, yes, did you see a lady in a brown dress with a white headscarf come past here? She was in the church when I went in."

The pretend vicar looked a little bemused.

"I'm sorry Sir, me and my colleague have been stood at the door since we opened and nobody dressed like that has been in the church. In fact we are a little surprised as only you and two others have been in and one of them was Mrs Cook who is in the Grove society. The other was a strangely dressed gentleman, he had plum coloured trousers with a bright yellow jacket and a checked shirt. He went in about two hours ago but had gone by the time you arrived."

Daniel didn't push it anymore for the fear of ridicule. He made his way back to the outside bar. It was now closed and Lee-Anne was cleaning down.

"You ok Daniel? You look like you have seen a ghost."

"I think I did Lee-Anne."

"What?"

"I have just been in the church and I saw Anouska. When I called her, she got up to leave. I followed and she appeared to walk through the church wall!"

"Well you do know there are troubled spirits, don't you?"

"What do you mean?"

"I have seen many in my time. They are people that have died sometimes horribly and they are not settled so they wander in the spirit world, hoping for contact with the living to alleviate there worries."

"Come on finish off helping me. Jeff has gone for the pick-up he will drop us off."

"We can open up tonight, then when the rest of the staff come on shift at 7.00pm we can go for a drink and I will explain."

Daniel finished wiping the glasses and bottling up. Then Jeff arrived and took everyone back to The Green Tankard. Daniel and Lee-Anne opened up, then staff arrived so they left for the night.

"Do you fancy a pizza Daniel in Logan's bar. They say they are out of this world?"

"Ok let's try it."

Logan's was quite a large building it had been a corn mill warehouse that had been converted in to business units, and Logan's had the first two floors. It was modelled on the American Tap House with over forty beers on tap and fridges full of every bottled beer you could imagine. Up the wrought iron stairs was an eating area. All the old red brick walls were exposed and they had rustic tables and chairs.

"This must have cost an arm and a leg to do up Lee-Anne."

"Yes, they really have made a nice job of it. Makes my little boozer seem irrelevant."

"No Daniel there is room in the market for both."

"Can we have table for two please?" Daniel requested of the waiter.

"Certainly Sir, follow me. Would this be alright Sir?"

The waiter had given them a seat which was like a balcony seat, they could watch all the people below.

"That's great, thank you."

"Would you like a drink to start with while you look at our excellent menu?"

Daniel took a quick look at the drinks menu. There was so many he decided to have a paddle, which was five different small beers on a paddle.

"Any preference Sir, or should I pick and mix for you?"

"That would be great."

"What would you like Madam?"

"Could I have large Chablis?"

"Not a problem, relax and I will fetch your drinks while you decide what you would like to eat."

"This is some menu Lee-Anne.

"I know. Look they have Boston Crab. I must have that to start. What about you Daniel?"

"I'm having the veal sweetbread."

"Don't even tell me where they come from Daniel," and she laughed. Daniel thought how nice it was that Lee-Anne had come back into his life. After losing Anouska and Jane she made him laugh which he needed. The waiter came back with the drinks. They told him their starters, then Lee-Anne ordered Pigeon Perigourdine with beetroot and a Romanesco sauce and truffle potatoes.

Daniel ordered fillet of veal on a bed of morels, broad beans and garlic. The waiter went off to place the order with the kitchen.

"Didn't realise the Americans ate so well Lee-Anne?"

"Not sure they do," and she laughed.

"What is your beer selection?"

"The cloudy one is called Big House and it's a Grapefruit Pale Ale. The next one is Amber Bock, a slightly darker ale number there is called Andrew Jackson Revenge. It's a dark malty beer."

"Great names Daniel."

"Aren't they just."

"Number four is JFK sweet ale?" Daniel paused for a minute and remembered his dream. Let's not ruin tonight he thought.

"Number five is Route 66. It says it's a light gritty beer whatever that means."

"Thank you," said Daniel and the waiter left with the orders.

"I dreamt I shot Kennedy, Lee-Anne."

"If you dreamt it you possibly did. It will be one of their tests Daniel. Let's try and forget all that for tonight."

Daniel knew Lee-Anne was right.

The meal arrived. There wasn't masses of it, but it was excellent quality. Over dinner Daniel told Lee-Anne about Amanda Cook from the Grove society, and said he was meeting her on Friday.

"Just be careful Daniel please."

"I will but she has some real interesting things. Harkan lived in Grove I saw his plaque. Apparently he was a preacher but went mad with fever and killed his children and his wife by cutting of their heads."

"That answers a few questions I think Daniel. Be careful please."

"I will Lee-Anne, don't worry."

"Now are we having a pudding?"

"Can we share?"

"Ok you choose."

Daniel chose the caramel and ginger roulade with Cornish clotted cream. They both tucked into the pudding, then Daniel paid the bill and walked Lee-Anne home. After seeing Anouska he didn't think it was right to ask her back to his. He kissed and

said goodnight, then walked the half
mile back to his house.

The week went well at the pub. At
home Daniel had no dreams and
began to quite look forward to his
meal with Amanda Cook, which was
that evening.

Daniel put on a nice blue suit with a
checked shirt and a light blue tie. He
got a taxi to Kempes restaurant. His
arrival was spot on as Amanda Cook
got out of her taxi at almost the same
time. Amanda had dark hair with big
hazel coloured eyes. She was wearing
a brown dress cut just above her knee
with a small cross that dangled
seductively on her chest. This was
complemented with some cream sling
back high heels.

The waiter showed them to their table.
The restaurant was quite busy, so a

good buzz of people having conversations. They ordered drinks and food and Amanda started to tell Daniel what she knew.

"It's been long believed Daniel, that Grove was the place of Evil. This stems back to your ancestor Dermot Egan and Leviathan Harkan. Harkan's first name means the devil did you know that?"

"No, I didn't Amanda."

Daniel had a decision to make. Did he tell her he knew Harkan? Looking back to his first meeting with him he deliberately spelt out his name to Daniel. So, he was telling him who he was.

Daniel decided to just let Amanda Cook talk and keep what he knew under his hat so to speak.

"Things happened back then that could have been to fever or anything. I mean they believed in witches, didn't they?"

Daniel almost choked on his dinner.

"You ok Daniel?"

"Yeah sorry, think a piece of Salmon went down the wrong way."

If only she knew he thought.

"Monk Gellycombe wrote that the crowd saw yellow bile coming out of McAndrew's mouth after an altercation with Dermot Egan. Where McAndrew actually died could have been the onset of fever, but because of Egan's fearsome reputation, they then said they saw Egan's eyes turn red. So I think the Monk was trying to say it wasn't the work of the devil. Just poorly educated people believing in something that wasn't there."

"The other incident the monk mentions is with the landlord of the pub in Grove, a certain William Brewster. He asked Dermot Egan to leave the ale house because he believed him to be a devil worshipper, and he was later found hung in the forest two days later. Again, the locals who saw the altercation said Dermot Egan's eyes turned blood red. The monk did write that Brewster's landlord had tripled his rent. He believed him to have money worries thus he hung himself."

Daniel thought the meeting was turning out to be a waste of time until Amanda Cook said she believed they were the work of a society called 'The Evil'. Daniel's ears pricked up.

"What makes you believe that Amanda?"

"I have done research on this and that got me interested. Oh, and I must say before I go much further, that it was no coincidence I met you. I have been researching you and your family ever since your wedding that never was, when those people collapsed and died with marks on their neck.

Daniel felt a bit uneasy with Amanda's latest revelation.

"I realise it's a bit cheeky of me Daniel but I thought if I got to know you, then you might open up on what you know about Harkan and your ancestor."

"I could tell you an awful lot, but you would either think I am nuts or by telling you it would put you in grave danger. Trust me I know."
"Daniel, I believe Harkan is alive today, and please don't bite my head off, but somehow Dermot Egan is

trying to live through you. Am I correct?"

"Look Amanda maybe this is the wrong place to have these discussions. Come to my house on Sunday and I will show some diaries."

"Daniel, I am married you know."

"No sorry Amanda, nothing like that but you said you believe these things so prepare yourself."

"Ok what time?"

"Say 11.00am."

Daniel gave her his address. Whilst doing it he wasn't sure if he should, but he just felt she had more to tell him.

They grabbed their coats. Daniel paid and they left in their respective taxis. Daniel arrived home and slept well that night, although it had been a strange night. The following day he was at work all day. He often wondered if Murdo would come in again but he hadn't so far, so he wasn't holding his breath.

The following morning Daniel tidied round ready for Amanda Cook to arrive. Spot on 11.00am the doorbell rang. Daniel answered it. Amanda Cook was standing on the doorstep and she looked a little nervous.

"Not sure if I should be doing this? Coming to basically a stranger's house on my own."

"Trust me Amanda, I am a good guy despite my ancestry," and he laughed which lightened the mood.

"Would you like some Eggs Benedict, I am having some."

"Oh, ok yes, that would be nice. My tummy has been in knots so I haven't eaten. I have dreamt of interviewing you about Grove for a while now. I can't believe you are giving me the opportunity."

"What I tell you cannot be written down or used in articles etc. Amanda."

"No, I promise it's just I need understanding."

Daniel served up their breakfast then questioned what she meant by understanding.

"Well I suppose I best tell you about me. I have never told anybody, not even my dear husband. This all started the day I read the report on the deaths at your wedding. That night I had a dream and I dreamt I was from Grove, but I was a serving wench. I worked at The Tumbling in a village called Socombe. I was the girl who McAndrew knew and he tried to protect me from Dermot. McAndrew's advance, it wasn't unusual for the men folk to get fruity with the serving wenches when they were full of ale. But this time it got out of hand. I actually believe I was there that day Daniel and Dermot Egan's eyes did turn red and after the altercation Malky. McAndrew did vomit like yellow bile, but it came out like a snake. It was about two inches in diameter and it came out about three feet long. It was awful, I screamed and dropped the ale. That was when I knew. On the side of McAndrew's neck I saw the same marks described in the Paisley Chronicles report on the deaths of your friends at the wedding. I knew that day I had to try and meet you.

"Did you dream anymore?"

"I did. One of my dreams in particular was disturbing. I was walking back to Grove from Socombe, and I know this sounds crazy, but I saw two witches. They were huddled in the forest chanting. I hid behind a tree as I was frightened they might see me. They had a big metal pot and they were throwing things in it. After about five minutes a massive red serpent reared from out of the pot opened its mouth to show its fangs, then it just disappeared. The two witches seemed happy at this, and they weren't like how witches are normally portrayed. They were only about thirty years old. As I hid in the bushes, they went passed me and I heard what they said."

"What was it they said?"

"Harkan has spoken and they were to put damnation on Grove, as it was 'The Evil's village now. I know this sounds ridiculous Daniel but I feel so much better I have told somebody about this."

"Right I believe you, I truly do. I will let you read my diary but not my granddad and mother's. But before you do, you are already in danger from Harkan and his sect for coming here today, and telling me what you have witnessed."

"Sit here. I will make you a coffee," and Daniel gave her his diaries to read. He carried on doing some pub work on his laptop. Amanda Cook took almost five hours to read what Daniel had written.

When she finally finished she said, "So are you going to save everyone Daniel, like the scroll said?"

"Look to be honest, I have lost everything dear to me with this stupid obsession and all it has brought me is heartache. I really just want to get on with my life."

"I am sorry Daniel. I can see that you are a nice man, but looking at this that maybe your downfall. 'The Evil' seem to think you have powers and one day it will all come to a head for you."

"I know my time is limited and whatever choice I make, I am sure they will have a twist in it. I just wish they would leave me alone, and this is all because of bloody Dermot Egan. So, what now for you Amanda?"

"Well since I saw you at Grove the dreams stopped, so I am hoping that Ellie Fairbury is at peace now. Did you see the Fairbury house was only one of three still half resembling a house? When I put the stake in the ground outside the house the day before the show I went really cold. Then had a blinding headache and I fainted. My husband brought me round. He put it down to doing too much and not eating, but I knew Ellie was trying to possess me. That village is evil Daniel. I do believe it is possessed, I really do."

"After reading your diaries I am heart-broken for you. It must be terrible and I only had the one worry of Ellie."

"I am trusting you not to repeat anything I have told you or you have read please."

"I won't Daniel, I promise." Amanda left Daniel thanking him for the breakfast and for sharing about Grove and the diaries.

Daniel immediately called Lee-Anne but there was no answer, it just kept going to answer phone on her mobile. After twenty tries he gave up and decided to go into work.

"Afternoon Jeff," he shouted as he passed the kitchen.

Jeff came out. "Are you ok Daniel?"

"Yes why?"

"Have you got a minute?"

"Of course mate, come down to my office. Take a seat mate what is it?"

Jeff could see Daniel didn't know.

"The police called round about twenty minutes ago. I tried to call your house phone but there was no answer and your mobile is switched off."

"It isn't Jeff. I never switch it off."

Daniel scrambled in his pocket and his mobile was switched off.

"That's odd Jeff don't know how that has happened. Anyway, what did the boys in blue want? They aren't banging on about us running over by twenty minutes on the music licence the other night are they?"

Jeff looked stunned.

"Are you ok mate?"

Jeff just blurted out, "She's dead Daniel."

"Whose dead?"

"Lee-Anne."

"What?"

"The police found her the car had gone off the road and hit a tree. I don't know how to tell you this Daniel, after your poor wife and child and what happened to them, but the police said she was decapitated."

Daniel sunk in his chair. How many more people will they kill? It was time to try and find Harkan once and for all. This can't go on he thought.

"Daniel, Daniel, here drink this." Jeff had a got a large brandy to help with the shock.

Daniel sipped his brandy and told the staff to shut the pub for the night as a mark of respect for Lee-Anne.

CHAPTER TWELVE

It was almost three months later, Daniel had buried Lee-Anne and things were getting back to normal. He had searched everywhere for Harkan but he knew deep down Harkan would find him eventually.

Daniel was sifting through his post when he found a letter addressed to a Mr Daniel Egan. On the back of the envelope was a return address. Should the letter not find Daniel, it simply said Return to Sender, Miss Amanda Cook, Thatched Cottage, Kally Wood, Nr Edinburgh.

He opened the letter and started to read.

'Dearest Daniel

GROVE

It was with massive regret that I heard of yet another loss for you. From what your diaries told me poor Lee-Anne was in the same circumstances as me, but there were also things I didn't understand about her.

You probably read my return address. I told something of a lie when I met you. I said I had a husband, this isn't true. I guess I used that scenario with coming to see you at your house and being a woman alone I felt a bit vulnerable.

The reason for me writing was not only to send my deepest sympathy to you, but to ask if you would like to visit me. I have some news I can't put in a letter.

This is my number;- 0061655 8899 62 and my address is on the envelope.

Please contact me, it is very important you do.

Yours sincerely

Amanda Cook'

Daniel thought this all very strange but he duly called Amanda Cook, and arranged to see her the following day.

Daniel drove out to Kally Wood near Edinburgh, which was a wood. He drove down a dirt track for almost a mile and eventually came to an isolated cottage with ivy growing on three sides. He knocked on the door, but when the door opened it was a very old lady.

"Oh, I am sorry. I was looking for Amanda Cook."

"Come in Daniel," the lady said. Daniel went inside the cottage on every wall were pictures of Grove.

"Sit down Daniel."

"Suddenly Daniel could see the piercing hazel coloured eyes of the lady in front of him, and he could detect Amanda's voice, which he had thought before that she had a bit of a Somerset accent.

"After I left you I drove home quite excited by our meeting. I thought I had met somebody that understood, and I know longer felt lonely with myself. About three days later there was a knock on my door. I never get visitors, that's why I bought this place. I opened the door and nearly fainted. It was Harkan. He barged his way in and ordered I make him a glass of milk. He slurped the milk with his big tongue dangling in the glass it was awful."

He looked at me and told me that I had been allowed to live because of my work with the Grove society, and while people thought there was evil there they would stay away. But he said I had done the show, and then subsequently met you. He even knew I had read your diaries. He said if I had read your Grandfather's and your Mothers he would bite me and take my head off. He said I was more use to him if I aged quickly and almost straight away I started aging Daniel. Amanda then started to cry. He has told me you are to meet him at the book store in Brook Street at midnight. He said he will be waiting. Before you go Daniel please do something for me."

"Anything Amanda?"

"Please kill me. Don't leave me like this, I beg you."

Amanda sat in the chair exhausted. She looked over a hundred years old and was aging in front of his eyes, but Daniel couldn't do it. Amanda appeared to fall asleep so he left.

He spent the rest of the day wandering round a park until almost midnight. He knew this was the time everyone had spoken off. '**Choice Time**.'

Brook Street was dimly lit. He passed a young couple kissing in one of the doorways, and arrived at the book shop. He tried the door and it opened with a creak. The shop had the old gas lights and it was quite dim at first until his eyes got used to the lack of bright light. As he walked through the entrance he felt something brush against him and it felt slimy.

Once inside the main shopping area Harkan was standing, smiling at him.

"What do you want Harkan, because trust me before I leave today I will kill you?"

Harkan laughed, "really you are a brave boy. Let me see now, what do I want?"

"I want your soul, and you will give it to my people."

"Why would I do that?"

"Sit down Daniel."

Daniel sat down in an old chair with rows of old dusty books behind him. As soon as he sat something slithered round him about twenty times to restrain him.

"What are you doing Harkan?"

"Just making sure I have your full attention."

"I will now explain the process you have been going through in some details; first your supposed dreams. Well let me put that myth to bed. They were not dreams, they were reality. Everything you dreamt you did and were actually there. These were a test to see if you were evil like your ancestor, or in fact you were here to supposedly save the human race from evil."

GROVE

At that, Harkan slithered his tongue out of his mouth wiping what looked like the remnants of his evening meal from his chin.

"Let's start with dream number one."

"You were William Dowd the nice little boy who failed in his task given to him by your ancestor Anthony Babington. He was later hung, drawn and quartered at St Giles Field near Holborn. Our verdict from this test: I was there Daniel watching you for 'The Evil'. My name was Leviathan Gifford. Funny how you never connected my name when I introduced myself to you over breakfast."

Harkan laughed.

"So, you allowed poor Babington to swing and history to carry on its course. To our mind a FAILURE."

"Dream two: Ah yes, good old butcher's apprentice Thomas Bent. When your master shared his secret for avoiding the plague you wrestled with your conscience, but you let your family die. So, for that we have a PASS."

"Dream three: We enjoyed this one the most. A chance to kill one of our prominent associates Adolf Hitler. Had you have done that you would have spared your mother the heartache of being Yochana, and would have changed the world forever. But we were pleased to see as young Harry Skills you let him go. So, from us that was another PASS."

"Dream Four: We decided to mix this up a bit. We felt that you may think these were just dreams and could tell people about them, but if we sent you time travelling you would not want to share this experience. You sat in a tree in Grove churchyard and were transported back to the time of your ancestor Dermot Egan. He is our ultimate master, who by the way has been very disappointed in your grandfather and your mother. He thought they would come over. They both killed, which was a good sign but both did this silly good thing, so we decided to dispense of them."

Daniel sat totally blown away with Harkan's knowledge of his life and others.

"Poor old Skillet, we really set him up. We knew he would want you to kill Dermot, and that was a big test. Could you kill known Evil, and you couldn't. Our verdict a massive PASS.

Dream Five: Oh yes Mr Stewey Lingfield and another chance to change the course of history. All those silly people for years thought Oswald was the killer. We even set up Jack Ruby to kill him to make it look like the mafia were stopping Oswald from talking. All the time it was us, 'The Evil' and you Stewey Lingfield, who killed that do gooder to further our aims. So, from our perspective a massive PASS."

"So, to summarise, four out of five passes is very good Daniel and we would like to welcome you to 'The Evil'. Would you like to say anything Daniel?"

Daniel remembered the pebble. He knew this was his only way out. He fumbled in his pocket but as he pulled it out, with the pebble being shiny, it slipped out of his hands. It slid across the wooden floor stopping

right in front of Harkan. Harkan
laughed.

"Oh yes, I see you have brought
your salvation along but if I remember
correctly you only have one travel
left. So let's kick that into touch," and
Harkan kicked the pebble away.

Damn Daniel thought.

"So, decision time Daniel. Not that
there is actually a decision to make,
but just to help you I am going to
introduce you to some people that
have helped us on the way.

"Come in Millie."

"Aunty Millie you ok?"

Millie walked in. She looked about
thirty with no shaking at all. She
didn't speak but her eyes were blood
red.

"Your aunty Millie, as you called
her, was so good it made me feel sick,
and we knew one day we would have
to deal with it. Adolf Hitler decided to

possess her. That's why the shaking started, and eventually good old Lee-Anne killed her."

"Lee-Anne?"

"Well in a roundabout way. You see Lee-Anne was evil at that time, but your bloody influence had started to change her. The day of your wedding she was instructed to kill all your guests but she stopped half-way through."

"You are saying Lee-Anne killed my best mate, and all those lovely people?"

"Yes, we had harsh words and we decided to make sure your baby wasn't born, or could have been born good and we would have another problem."

"My next guest is good old Murdo, your buddy. Come in Murdo."

Murdo walked in the room. He looked terrified.

"Come and stand with me Murdo, that's it just there."

"Murdo was useful initially, getting the diaries etc but I am afraid he told you too much."

Quick as a flash Harkan's tongue wrapped round Murdo's neck and he stood paralysed. Harkan then picked a Samurai sword up and with one clean swoop decapitated Murdo's head from his torso. Daniel was almost sick.

"You see Daniel, Murdo was running with the hare and the hound and we can't have that. Hence the lovely Lee-Anne was doing the same. She was evil but after you gave her the stupid pebble she changed, so she had to die."

Daniel was praying this was another stupid dream. Murdo's body did not emit any blood!

"What about my wife and daughter?"

"Well nothing we could do there. They had to die just in case you made the wrong decision today, and had you still had family you may have stayed to fight 'The Evil'."

"Now you have nothing to stop you joining us, you can meet the master. A man in the dream in sack cloth with a hood covering his face appeared. Suddenly the snake like thing that had been restraining him let go.

"Good evening Daniel, or should I say early morning. Let me tell you something before we are done here. Amanda Cook aged to almost 400 hundred years and her bones just crumbled, so she won't be bothering us again."

"Mr Harkan is a loyal servant of 'The Evil' as is your Aunty Millie now, aren't you Millie?"

Millie nodded, she seemed able to talk and move now. She looked at Daniel and gestured to the sword as all the attention was on Dermot Egan. Daniel grabbed the sword and swung it decapitating Harkan.

Harkan's head rolled on the floor. In a matter of seconds he was back. Hs whole body turned into a massive red serpent.

"Leave this to me Harkan," Dermot Egan shouted.

"Ok Daniel, that was a bit silly. You can't kill us you see. Only converts are vulnerable, like your Aunty Millie. Watch."

He launched the sword at Millie who screamed as her head left her body, and she dropped to the floor.

"Fancy thinking I would not see her little gesture to you a moment ago."

"You are only alive now Daniel because you are an Egan, and I believe you will take my place eventually. Now it really is choice time. Do I have a Yes or a No?"

Daniel made his move for the pebble but Dermot Egan picked him up with his scaly hands. I take that as a no then Daniel. With one swoop he swung the sword. Daniel tried to protect himself. He shouted, "Damn you." The sword severed his arm, then Dermot Egan swung again decapitating Daniel.

GROVE

Dermot Egan smiled and turned to
Harkan, who by now resembled a
serpent.

"These stupid people think they are
protected from us. It's a shame,
Daniel had to die he would have been
a great successor ….

GROVE

You have been on a roller coaster ride through Goodness and Evil. Joy and Sorrow. Hope and Despair.

Now you have read this book possibly the next time you dream perhaps you are being coached for 'The Evil' or will you think they are just what the ordinary person puts them down too dreams or nightmares.

Who knows what the characters in the three books had been subject to? Were they dreaming, or having a nightmare, or were they there and this parallel world really exists for some people.

Déjà Vie and unexplained dreams are something we all experience in our lives at some point.

Maybe now you may think differently.

GROVE

 Our dreams can shape our lives or can they shape our death.

You decide!

C J Galtrey is a successful published author who is published on different genres with the following books available on Amazon throughout the world.

John Gammon Peak District Detective books.

Follow DI Gammon in his professional and personal life played out to the back drop of the Peak District National Park, and see what places you may have visited and maybe met some of the characters.

Book One: **Things Will Never Be The Same Again**

Book Two: **Sad Man**

GROVE

Book Three: **Joy Follows Sorrow**

Book Four: **Never Cry On A Bluebell**

Book Five: **Annie Tanney**

Book Six: **The Poet And The Calling Card**

Book Seven: **Why**

Book Eight: **Your Past Is Your Future**

Book One in The John Gammon series 'Things Will Never Be The Same Again' is available in E Format, Paperback and now on Audio with Amazon, Audible.com and I Tunes.

The Looking For Shona Trilogy are books with Romance, History, Happiness, Sadness and Time Travel

Book One: **Looking For Shona**

Book Two: **The Hurt of Yochana**

Book Three: **Grove**

A book which is about a girl on the run. This book is based in London, Cornwall and Derbyshire.

Got To Keep Running.

See all the books on my web site www.colingaltrey.co.uk

On the web site there are book links that will take you to Amazon to purchase in E Format or Paperback

GROVE

Printed in Germany
by Amazon Distribution
GmbH, Leipzig

17212049R00233